'You manipul[ative...]' [she] breathed.

Simon didn't den[y it. A mocking smile] twisted the corners of his mouth and he returned her gaze with a frank, admiring appraisal. Tension flared between them like voltage travelling along a wire. Holly was suddenly conscious of the steamy heat in the hallway, of the overpowering fragrance of roses that was making her head swim. And, worse still, of some other nameless and far more potent force...

Dear Reader

Summer is here at last...! And what better way to enjoy these long, long days and warm romantic evenings than in the company of a gorgeous Mills & Boon hero? Even if you can't jet away to an unknown destination with the man of your dreams, our authors can take you there through the power of their storytelling. So pour yourself a long, cool drink, relax, and let your imagination take flight...

The Editor

Angela Devine grew up in Tasmania surrounded by forests, mountains and wild seas, so she dislikes big cities. Before taking up writing, she worked as a teacher, librarian and university lecturer. As a young mother and Ph.D. student, she read romantic fiction for fun and later decided it would be even more fun to write it. She is married with four children, loves chocolate and Twinings teas and hates ironing. Her current hobbies are gardening, bushwalking, travelling and classical music.

Recent titles by the same author:

THE BRIDE OF SANTA BARBARA

MISSISSIPPI MOONLIGHT

BY
ANGELA DEVINE

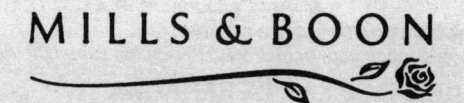

MILLS & BOON

MILLS & BOON LIMITED
ETON HOUSE, 18-24 PARADISE ROAD
RICHMOND, SURREY TW9 1SR

To Erin with love

DID YOU PURCHASE THIS BOOK WITHOUT A COVER?

If you did, you should be aware it is **stolen property** as it was reported *unsold and destroyed* by a retailer. Neither the Author nor the publisher has received any payment for this book.

All the characters in this book have no existence outside the imagination of the Author, and have no relation whatsoever to anyone bearing the same name or names. They are not even distantly inspired by any individual known or unknown to the Author, and all the incidents are pure invention.

All Rights Reserved. The text of this publication or any part thereof may not be reproduced or transmitted in any form or by any means, electronic or mechanical, including photocopying, recording, storage in an information retrieval system, or otherwise, without the written permission of the publisher.

This book is sold subject to the condition that it shall not, by way of trade or otherwise, be lent, resold, hired out or otherwise circulated without the prior consent of the publisher in any form of binding or cover other than that in which it is published and without a similar condition including this condition being imposed on the subsequent purchaser.

MILLS & BOON and the Rose Device are trademarks of the publisher.

First published in Great Britain 1994 by Mills & Boon Limited

© Angela Devine 1994

Australian copyright 1994   Philippine copyright 1994
This edition 1994

ISBN 0 263 78578 5

Set in Times Roman 10 on 11 pt.
01-9408-58286 C

Made and printed in Great Britain

CHAPTER ONE

'GO SEE who's at the door, honey. That guy's goin' to break it down if you don't!'

Holly looked up at the elderly black woman and gave an exasperated sigh. Sophie was right. The knocking at the front door of the tiny restaurant had stopped. But now the customer had gone round to the courtyard at the rear and was hammering furiously at the entrance to the back porch as if he really did intend to break it down. Holly pushed a damp ginger curl off her hot forehead with her knuckles, swept a pile of moist, pink shrimps and fresh chopped parsley into the simmering pan on the stove and then gave the mixture a practised swirl with the wooden spoon before tasting it. A medley of powerful aromas and flavours filled her nostrils. Garlic, tomato, celery, lemon, green pepper, tabasco. And, of course, the seafood. Well, if the shrimp Creole at La Crevette wasn't up to standard tonight, it wouldn't be her fault. Even if she had been expected to put up with a lunatic breaking the door down while she worked. The thunderous knocking started again.

'Can't he read?' grumbled Holly, turning down the gas and wiping her hands on her apron. 'The "CLOSED" sign is on the door, for heaven's sake!'

With swift, impatient steps she marched out to the back porch, trying to remind herself to handle the problem just the way Heather would. After all, this idiot was a potential customer and she didn't want to drive him away forever, only until six p.m. But the truth was that Holly didn't resemble her sister a bit, except in looks. Where Heather was shy, reserved and tactful, Holly was blunt, spirited and had a temper like a nuclear warhead. Diplomacy came as naturally to her as it would to a Bengal tiger. Picking her way between the dustbins and the cleaning implements that cluttered the back porch, she jerked on the blind that covered the glass door and got ready to smile. Unfortunately the blind shot skywards and wound itself violently round and round the cylinder.

'Damn!' cried Holly.

'Don't stand there cursing. Let me in!' ordered a furious voice from outside.

For the first time Holly saw him clearly. He was quite tall, at least six feet, probably in his mid thirties, with dark, glossy hair and the fiercest navy blue eyes she had ever seen. And, of all things, he was wearing a suit. A suit! In New Orleans, in the heat of summer! That settled it. He was definitely crazy. Either that or he had no normal human responses to anything, including weather and 'CLOSED' signs on restaurant doors. Holly gave him a sugar-sweet smile and with big, exaggerated movements pointed to the sign hanging on the door.

'Sorry. We're closed until six o'clock,' she said very loudly and brightly.

'Open this door or I swear I'll rip it off the hinges,' he retorted.

Holly blinked. Was he really some kind of madman? Yet even through the glass, his voice held a resonant, commanding quality. And he didn't actually look insane. Just very, very angry. In fact, now that she thought about it, his whole body and manner seemed totally out of keeping with the clothes he wore. His suit was grey, lightweight, beautifully cut and completely in accord with the crisp, white shirt and striped blue tie which accompanied it. It was the outfit of a conservative, controlled businessman. But there was nothing conservative or controlled about the man inside it. In spite of his neatly trimmed hair and smoothly shaven shin, he had an aura of wildness and untamed urgency about him, as if he would let nothing stand in his way in order to get what he wanted. With a strong sense of misgiving, she pulled the bolts, drew open the door and stood back. It was just as well she did, for the newcomer surged into the room with the irresistible force of a lava flow.

'All right. What the hell is going on here?' he demanded.

'Nothing is going on!' snapped Holly.

The man laughed harshly.

'Well, that's apparent!' he sneered. 'Nothing at all. But it should be. I've been waiting at my house for you since three o'clock, but there hasn't been a sign of you.'

Holly's mouth hung open.

'I-I'm sorry,' she said in bewilderment. 'But what exactly are you talking about?'

The stranger gave an exasperated snort.

'I'm talking about the dinner for thirty people which you're supposed to be serving in my house at eight o'clock tonight! Did you or did you not take a telephone booking three weeks ago to cater for a party at my house tonight?'

Holly opened her mouth to deny the charge indignantly. Three weeks ago!

'I wasn't even in New Orleans——' she began.

And then stopped as an appalling thought struck her. It was true. She hadn't been in New Orleans then, but Heather had. And it was just about the time that Holly's sister had been rushed to hospital after an accident in the restaurant. Nobody had been with her when she was hurt and it had never been quite clear how it had happened. All they knew was that Sophie, arriving at three in the afternoon, had found Heather unconscious on the kitchen floor with a broken leg and a lump on her head. It was obvious that she had slipped in some soup that had boiled over on the stove and dripped on the floor, although nobody knew why. But what if Heather had taken a telephone booking, heard the soup boiling over and rushed into the kitchen to turn it off without writing any message down? Holly experienced a sinking sensation in the pit of her stomach as if she had just dropped ten floors in a lift.

'It's possible that there was a booking,' she admitted warily. 'Although I didn't take it. May I ask your name please, sir?'

There was another impatient snort from the stranger.

'My name's the same as it was on the last two occasions you did catering for me, Miss Thomson!' he snarled. 'Simon Madigan. And the address is the same too—Chartres House on the Great River Road. You ought to remember, seeing you had a flat tyre in that old green van of yours last time you came out there!'

Holly hid a reluctant grin. Yes, the mention of the old green van clinched it. He definitely had her confused with Heather. It was a problem they had suffered since they were teenagers. Not that they were twins or anything, but they were both short and sturdy with remarkably similar voices. And having the same flaming ginger curls didn't help matters. Wincing, Holly tried to adopt the soothing manner that came so easily to her sister.

'I'm sorry,' she said. 'There's obviously been some mistake——'

'You're damned right there has and you've made it! Why weren't you at my house on the dot of three o'clock the way you promised? You've made me waste a lot of my valuable time looking for you.'

His anger seemed to radiate out in waves to attack her. It smouldered around the edges of his dark blue eyes and in the aggressive set of his mouth. Even the stance of his body issued a furious challenge. Muscular legs were planted wide apart with a slight crouch at the knees. Lean brown hands rested threateningly on narrow hips as if he were reaching for a pair of six shooters.

And his chin jutted forward at a dangerous angle. In spite of herself, Holly felt an unwilling thrill at this blatant masculine antagonism. Yet her own reaction made her bristle with resentment. She was here in New Orleans to help Heather, not to have irrational physical responses to strange men!

'Why didn't you telephone when nobody arrived?' she asked tartly.

'I did. But your telephone doesn't work, like everything else around this place.'

'What?' demanded Holly. 'It was fine at lunchtime. I used it. I just can't believe it!'

With brisk, impatient steps she rushed through the steamy kitchen, past the astonished Sophie into the restaurant itself. The telephone looked exactly as always. A handsome brass and wood reproduction antique, bought to complement the décor of the old fashioned room, it sat on the countertop next to a brass cash register by the front door. Holly threaded her way between the black bentwood chairs, the tiny tables with their snowy white lace tablecloths and the luxuriant green plants that occupied every spare corner. But, as she darted behind the counter, her foot caught in the gap between the black and white checkerboard tiles on the floor, and she almost pitched headlong into the battered walnut piano. In fact she would have done if the stranger had not seized her arm to steady her. She caught her breath, suddenly conscious of the strength in those lean brown fingers and of the clean, spicy tang of aftershave which emanated from his body. To her annoyance, she felt her heartbeat accelerate.

'Thank you,' she said primly, pulling herself free. 'I keep forgetting that tile is broken.'

'You ought to get it fixed,' warned the stranger. 'That's really quite dangerous. The local government authority could close you down for something like that.'

'I realise that,' retorted Holly with an edge to her voice. 'And I've already tried to get somebody to fix it. In the meantime we're just going to have to be careful. In any case, only our staff ever come into this area. Now if you'll excuse me I'll just check the telephone.'

She picked up the phone and listened. There was no doubt about it. It was completely dead. The only sounds she could hear were the creak and swish of the ceiling fan overhead and the sudden loud sizzling from the kitchen as Sophie cooked a new load of shrimps.

'Convinced?' asked the stranger in a mocking tone.

Holly held on to her temper.

'Yes, thank you,' she replied. 'I'm sorry you've had so much trouble trying to contact me, Mr Madigan. I'll go out and phone the telephone company in a moment to check what happened.'

He shrugged impatiently.

'I already did,' he said. 'Apparently there are builders working next door. They backed their truck into the telegraph pole and brought down all the lines for this entire city block. The repairman should be over any time now to fix it.'

A brief, wry smile touched Holly's lips.

'Well, that's a relief!' she exclaimed. 'At least there's something that's not my fault. Now about these bookings for your dinner party. I think I can explain——'

Simon held up his hand imperiously like a policeman stopping traffic.

'I don't have time to listen to any explanations. I have other things to do. Can you or can't you produce a meal at my place at eight tonight?'

Holly winced. Could she? It was a pretty tall order, especially considering that she didn't even know where the house was, what was on the menu, or who she would have to help her. Not to mention the tiny problem that she had a restaurant to run as well. But Holly was nothing if not impulsive.

'Of course I can!' she said. 'No problems... although if you could just tell me the menu you had in mind that would help.'

Simon looked at her as if she were half witted.

'The menu?' he echoed. 'You mean you don't even remember that? Look, never mind, I'll go elsewhere. I thought you were pretty capable, but obviously I was wrong. Of course, you needn't expect any more business from me in the future.'

And he swung on his heel as if to leave.

'Wait!' cried Holly with such passion that he stopped in his tracks and turned back to look at her. 'I'll do it. I promise I'll do it! I'll even give you a money-back guarantee. If you aren't satisfied with the dinner, you don't pay a thing. How's that? All you need to do is tell me what the menu was.'

Simon's black eyebrows drew together in a thoughtful frown and his blue eyes assessed Holly from head to foot.

'Shrimp Creole, duck á l'orange, butter pecan cheesecake with caramel sauce,' he muttered under his breath. 'But are you sure you're up to this, Miss Thomson? From what I've seen today, you don't strike me as being very capable.'

Holly's freckled face flamed.

'I'm a qualified chef with four years' experience from the best hotels in the United States and Australia!' she said in a taut, angry voice. 'And whatever else I may be, I'm a damned good cook, Mr Madigan.'

Simon was still watching her assessingly out of those half closed blue eyes.

'It's not just the cooking,' he said. 'It's a silver service dinner. You'll need to be dressed better than that to serve it.'

For the first time Holly glanced down at herself and became aware of what she was wearing. It was all she could do not to groan aloud. Without even noticing it, she had put on an apron given to her as a graduation present by some of the male chefs in her class, a lavish affair depicting a half naked woman in a red frilly G-string. Horrified, Holly snatched it off and shoved it under the counter. Not that the result was much better. Underneath it she was wearing a T shirt and shorts, both liberally splashed with tomato purée and with long, smeary fingerprints where she had wiped her hands on them. Holly might be a good cook, but she was undoubtedly a messy one.

'Oh, that's a great improvement.'

'Don't worry, I'll change before I come,' cried Holly. 'Give me the address and I'll drive up there as soon as I've packed up my equipment.'

He hesitated for a moment and then appeared to reach a decision. To her surprise, he suddenly seized her by the shoulders. His warm fingers seemed to scorch through the thin cotton of her T shirt and his face was thrust so close to hers that she could see the tiny pattern of lines around the corners of his eyes.

'All right,' he growled. 'I'll give you a chance. But I'm going to make damned sure you don't let me down again, so there's no way I'll let you drive out alone to my place. Right now I've got other things to do here in the city, important things, but I'll be back in half an hour to pick you up. And I'm warning you, I want everything perfect tonight. The menu exactly as we agreed, the service faultless and you looking like the owner of a decent restaurant, instead of a refugee from a vampire's birthday party. And no more disasters. Do I make myself clear?'

'Yes,' snapped Holly.

'Good,' said Simon, releasing her abruptly. 'Because I've no intention of being made to look a fool in front of my guests. Now do you really think you can manage this?'

'Yes,' insisted Holly fervently. 'Everything will be perfect. I promise.'

'It had better be,' retorted Simon, heading for the door. 'Otherwise I'll make you wish you'd never been born!'

Inevitably the brass door catch jammed as he tried to open it. Holly raced across the room, ducked under his arm and wrenched it free. One look at his thunderous face told her that he was not impressed. A jolt of antagonism like a two-hundred-and-forty-volt current lanced from those amazing blue eyes as he strode past her.

'Have a nice day,' she cooed after him.

But her defiant humour didn't last long. The moment the door had closed behind his departing back, Holly collapsed into a bentwood chair, stared at the wall and let out a low groan. Simon's hostility had worked on her just the way her brother's goading had when she was a child. Even as a nine-year-old she had never been able to resist a dare, and for some reason her thoughts winged back to her very first swimming race. Mike had entered her in a hundred-yard freestyle sprint, knowing perfectly well that she couldn't even swim ten in spite of her boasting. With a shudder Holly recalled her feelings as she'd climbed on to the starting blocks. Terror that she was going to flounder and then drown, an unwillingness to admit that she couldn't really do it and a dogged determination to make it come right somehow. Funny how nothing seemed to have changed in the last seventeen years! She groaned again.

'What have I done?' she demanded aloud. 'What have I done?'

Sophie padded grumbling in from the kitchen, with a tray containing two large glasses of iced tea. She looked about her in surprise.

'Wasn't that Mr Madigan?' she asked. 'Where is he? Has he gone already?'

Holly snatched up one of the glasses and took a long, reviving swallow of the bittersweet lemon-flavoured drink.

'Yes, it was,' she agreed. 'And he has. You'd better sit down and have the other drink, Sophie; you're going to need it.'

Sophie stared at her in alarm.

'What you done now, honey?' she demanded in alarm. 'It's something bad, ain't it?'

Holly took another gulp of the iced tea and looked at her guiltily.

'Not exactly,' she replied. 'I just took a booking from Mr Madigan to cater for a dinner of thirty people—silver service.'

Sophie beamed. Lowering herself heavily into one of the bentwood chairs, she spooned sugar into her iced tea.

'Well, that's wonderful, honey,' she said encouragingly. 'Miss Heather sure will be pleased. She needs every last cent she can get, what with these hospital bills and the parish wanting her to do building repairs and everything. When is this dinner, honey?'

Holly cleared her throat.

'Tonight,' she said.

Sophie's teaspoon clattered to the floor.

'Tonight!' she exclaimed. 'How in the name of heaven do you think we can do that, Miss Holly? That ain't possible!'

'It's got to be possible, Sophie!' cried Holly. 'Listen, just listen. What happened was this, or at least I think it was. Simon Madigan must have called up Heather and made a booking just before she got hurt. She didn't enter it in the bookings notebook, so I knew nothing about it until now. And he's counting on me to produce a meal at eight o'clock tonight for thirty people. If I don't do it, he'll never ask Heather to cater for anything again.'

Sophie sighed.

'Well, that's true,' she admitted. 'And Mr Madigan was mighty generous last time she worked for him. Besides, he's one of the most important men in New Orleans. Oh, lord! We're in a real spot.'

Holly jumped to her feet and paced restlessly round the tiny room.

'I think we can manage it, Sophie,' she urged persuasively. 'I'm sure I can handle the cooking at Mr Madigan's house if you can just cope here. Maybe we can call someone up and ask them to come in and help you?'

Sophie looked doubtful.

'Well, I guess my sister Emmeline could do it,' she admitted. 'She was here working with me for a few days before you flew in from Hawaii. Although she ain't half the cook you are, Miss Holly.'

Holly stopped her pacing and hugged the older woman warmly.

'You're a peach, Sophie! It will only be for one night. And it would mean so much to Heather if we can manage it. Do you really think we can?'

Sophie gave a wheezy chuckle.

'Well, you've already decided, haven't you?' she demanded. 'So I guess it ain't no use talking. We better get to working, honey. What you going to feed those people at Madigan's place?'

Good question, thought Holly five minutes later. She was standing in front of the huge refrigerator in the kitchen, chewing her lip and staring into its chilly interior. Luckily the big pot of Shrimp Creole was already cooked, so she could take that with her. And as fate would have it, she had made three butter pecan cheesecakes only the night before. If she cut the portions a little smaller than usual, those should serve ten people, although it left no allowance for accidents or second helpings. And what about the ducks? Where on earth was she to find enough ducks to feed thirty people at this hour of the day? She looked down at her watch and heaved a deep sigh. Seven minutes to five. Then she remembered that the poulterer's shop where they bought all their ducks didn't close until six o'clock. Maybe if she made a telephone call and ordered some... No, the telephone was out of order. Well, it was only two blocks away. Could she run over there?

Two minutes later she was out on the footpath, head down, elbows pumping, racing through the French Quarter of the city, barely aware of the sauntering crowds in their brightly coloured clothes, of the jazz music blaring out from bars, of the air that lay like a hot, damp blanket on her skin. At last she staggered to a halt in the poultry shop, gasped out an incoherent explanation and was promised an immediate delivery of eight ducks. Then she set off again. This time it was four blocks in the other direction to her sister's tiny apartment. There was no time to shower and change as she would have liked, but she dragged an elegant black dress of Heather's off its hanger, flung it into a plastic carrier bag with a gold brooch, a pair of black stockings and a pair of high-heeled pumps and set off again. Halfway down the stairs she remembered her niece Amber, who was being cared for by neighbours, but there was no time even to stop in and say hello to her. All she could do was jog frantically back to the restaurant, feeling hotter and sweatier with each passing minute.

She made it, but only just. When Simon returned at five twenty-three, Holly was stuffing a string bag full of oranges into a huge cardboard carton, already laden with eight ducks, a bag of fresh vegetables, and a pot of Shrimp Creole. A second equally gigantic carton held various cooking utensils, Holly's chef's outfit and the three precious cheesecakes wrapped in waxed paper and stored on protective trays. As Simon materialised beside her, looking cool and composed in his business suit,

Holly jumped. He had come through the back entrance so silently that she had not even heard him approach.

'All ready? If you'll just open the doors I'll carry these out to the car.'

Holly hurried to open the French doors leading to the street, and Simon hoisted up one of the enormous cartons as if it weighed nothing and led the way outside. A shiny, dark blue Mercedes was parked next to the kerb with its boot already open. Simon deposited the first carton inside, and returned for the second one. As he was lifting it, Holly gave a startled yelp.

'Just a minute! Just a minute!' she shouted. 'I've forgotten something.'

Darting across to the bar, she picked up a bottle of Curaçao and ran after him, pushing it into the overloaded carton just as he reached the street. But she had forgotten that the string bag containing the oranges was already torn. The movement dislodged a cascade of the fruit, which hit the bottle of liqueur. The Curaçao wobbled precariously, fell to the pavement and smashed.

'Oh, no!' wailed Holly, kneeling down beside it, and snatching wildly at some large pieces of glass.

'Stop that!' ordered Simon sternly. 'You'll cut yourself.'

'But I can't just leave it,' gabbled Holly. 'Someone might get hurt. And I don't know if I've got another bottle in the restaurant. What am I going to do?'

'Stop panicking for a start,' growled Simon. 'I've got some Curaçao at the house if you need it for cooking. And I'll soon have this cleaned up for you.'

He strode calmly across to the building next door where a workman in shorts and a navy singlet was removing a window frame with a hammer and chisel. Simon spoke to him in a low voice, a twenty-dollar bill changed hands, and the workman nodded respectfully.

'Sure thing, sir. Be glad to.'

A moment later the workman had abandoned his hammer and chisel and was walking towards them with a dustpan and brush. Simon held open the back door of the car for Holly.

'Get in,' he ordered.

Wishing that the ground would open up and swallow her, Holly obeyed. When she had fumbled her way into the seatbelt, she suddenly realised that she was not alone in the car. She had a muddled impression of a tall, elegant, blonde woman clad in a chic navy dress, regarding her with sardonic amusement from the front seat. Then Simon opened the driver's door and climbed inside.

'Virginia, I'd like you to meet Heather Thomson, who's catering for our dinner tonight. Miss Thomson, this is Virginia Cox, a college professor from upstate New York who's here to research a book on eighteenth century Louisiana. She's also doing some statistical analysis for me.'

Holly opened her mouth to protest about her name, but then realised that Virginia was extending five elegantly manicured fingers across the seat to her. Flustered, Holly clutched them and shook them.

'How do you do?' she began, then broke off. 'Oh, I'm awfully sorry. It's the Curaçao. I didn't realise my hands were so sticky!'

Virginia gave her a pained look and withdrew her fingers, rubbing them together fastidiously.

'Yes, of course,' she said.

Holly subsided miserably, and was relieved when the other woman turned her attention back to Simon. For the first time in years she felt like an apprentice chef again. Clumsy, apprehensive, eager to please but fearful of failing. The sensation annoyed her. The trouble was that Simon Madigan had caught her completely by surprise. She knew that she was impulsive, a bit untidy, given to sudden brainwaves and unforeseen disasters. But she wasn't normally either clumsy or unreliable. And yet now he was clearly convinced that she was both. Not that he intended to let it bother him one bit, she could see that. As far as Simon Madigan was concerned, Holly was obviously just some kind of rather unsatisfactory servant whose incompetence he had to endure for a single evening. And it wouldn't ruffle his composure a bit. Not a bit! Even if she served the ducks raw, he would still look down his long, aristocratic nose with that bored expression, lift one black, indolent eyebrow and demand something else. He wouldn't even care enough to get really annoyed with her. And yet he did have a temper. A fugitive smile twitched the corners of Holly's mouth as she remembered how he had caught her by the shoulders as he recited his list of conditions for the dinner. There was something very, very physically disturbing about being held by Simon Madigan... did it get even more disturbing if he kissed you?

With a horrified jolt, Holly sat back in her seat and reined in her unruly thoughts. Instead she tried to make sense of the conversation that Simon and Virginia were having in the front seat. Their talk washed over her in meaningless waves. A lot of stuff about the Stock Exchange and the Dow Jones Index. A few references to the Acadian French settlers driven out of Canada by the British in 1755. And something about new markets opening up in eastern Europe. Holly gathered that Simon's business had something to do with the production of CDs and cassettes, especially CDs of local jazz and Cajun music. Normally that would have fascinated her, since Holly was an enthusiastic jazz fan, but at the moment she felt too preoccupied to care. All she could think of was her fierce need to prove herself tonight, to make the dinner really successful so that Simon Madigan would have to look at her with respect. She'd show him a thing or two and make him admit that she was damned good at her job. After that, she never wanted to see him again!

The French Quarter, with its iron lace balconies, its wrought-iron street lamps, its hanging masses of greenery, and its shifting throng of brightly dressed inhabitants, slipped away behind them. Now they were in the more affluent part of the city, with gracious houses surrounded by magnolias and live oaks. More suburbs flashed by. And then they reached open country, green, hot and steamy, with occasional glimpses of paddle steamers on the river. At last Simon turned the car off into an avenue lined with oak trees, which led to one of the most magnificent houses that Holly had ever seen. It was a Greek revival mansion, with six white pillars at the front, three storeys high surmounted by a cupola. Holly caught her breath in admiration at the sight of it, but Simon and Virginia went on talking as if nothing special had happened. Then Simon drove around to the rear of the house and stopped the car on a brick patio. Climbing out, he opened Holly's door, and looked down at her with a smile that didn't quite reach his eyes.

'Well, here we are,' he said in a tone that held an unmistakable challenge. 'Now's your chance to put things right, Miss Thomson.'

CHAPTER TWO

Two minutes later Holly found herself standing in the sort of kitchen she had always dreamed of owning. It was a cook's paradise. A room twenty feet long and almost as wide, with mahogany cupboards and wide Corian countertops running all the way around the walls. Whisper-soft air-conditioning made the place as cool as an Eskimo's igloo and a faint, pleasant aroma of lemon and cedar rose from a cut-glass bowl of pot pourri set under one window. The red glow of the setting sun slanted through the glass and winked off the gleaming surface of every imaginable appliance. There was a double-bowled sink, dishwasher and microwave oven, huge refrigerator/freezer, a wall oven, and a host of electrical gadgets. In the centre of the room, under a vast copper hood, an island bench held a gas cooktop, and an auxiliary sink for washing vegetables. With a jerk of his head Simon indicated a swing door in one wall.

'This is a formal meal tonight, so we'll eat in the dining-room, not on the patio the way we did last time. If you need anything, just ask Letty Edwards. But of course you've been here before so you should know your own way around. I'll leave you to it. Don't disappoint me, will you?'

And before Holly could say another word, he strode out of the room. Her first impulse was to run after him, plant herself in his way and demand that he listen to her explanation. But she was foiled by the arrival of a grey-haired man carrying the first of her cartons and wanting to know where he should put it. He wiped his right hand on his jeans before extending it to Holly, introduced himself as Bob Edwards and said he'd heard all about her from his wife.

'Y-you mean Letty Edwards?' stammered Holly. 'Is she the housekeeper?'

Bob gave her a strange look.

'Yeah. I thought you met her last time you were here? I was out at the hardware store that day but Letty told me all about you.'

'Well, I——'

'Look, it don't matter. I got to rush, honey. There's the rest of your gear to bring in and then I have to change my clothes. I'm bartending tonight.'

Before Holly could reply, he vanished in search of the other carton. She was just running her fingers through her hair in a dazed fashion when, true to Simon's promise, the housekeeper appeared through the swing door from the dining-room. She advanced towards Holly with both hands held out and a beaming smile on her face.

'Why, Heather, honey,' she began. And then stopped with an expression of comic disbelief on her face. 'Now, hold on a minute! You're not Heather, are you?'

Holly gave a relieved gulp of laughter.

'No! And I'm glad somebody realises it. I've been having trouble getting Mr Madigan to believe me. You see——'

And rapidly she explained. Halfway through, Mrs Edwards flung up her hands and gave a gasp of laughter.

'Well, if that ain't just like a man! Blind in one eye and can't see out of the other. And Mr Simon don't like to be told that he's made a mistake, neither. You take my advice, honey. Keep your lips zipped, get this dinner on the table, and explain to him later. He ain't in no mood to listen to you right now.'

It was good advice, and Holly took it. In any case, she had too much to do to waste time talking. It was now after six-thirty and she would have to hurry if dinner were to be ready by eight o'clock. Once she had scrambled into her white chef's coat and hat, Holly's confidence began to return. Deftly she began melting butter and browning the ducks, using four heavy iron pans at the same time for greater speed. When all the birds were safely in the oven and a heavenly aroma of roast duck was filling the air, she took a break to consider her strategy.

'Right. Now, Mrs Edwards, can you tell me about the dining-room arrangements? I'll need to set the table and so on.'

The housekeeper smiled.

'Call me Letty, honey,' she urged. 'And don't you worry none about that. I got everything under control. Just come and look.'

She led Holly into the dining-room and gave a satisfied smile at her low gasp of admiration. Holly's parents owned a restaurant in Hawaii, and she was used to attractively decorated tables, but she had never seen anything to equal this. Everything in the room proclaimed a love of traditional good quality. The mahogany table was covered in a starched white double damask tablecloth which provided a perfect background to Wedgwood china, polished silver, fine crystal wine glasses and a magnificent silver épergne filled with orange lilies. The rest of the room revealed the same discreetly opulent taste with its avocado-coloured walls, vast chandelier, ornately decorated fireplace and precisely arranged oil paintings on the walls. These seemed to depict generations of Simon's ancestors and, while fashions in clothing had obviously changed, one thing had not: the haughty blue-eyed stare with which the men of this family confronted the world.

'It's real pretty, ain't it?' demanded Mrs Edwards with justifiable pride.

'Yes,' agreed Holly, but a troubled frown knitted her forehead. The room was beautiful, nobody could dispute that, and yet somehow it oppressed her spirits too. 'But somehow you can't imagine anybody eating pizza or watching TV in it or kicking their shoes off, can you?'

Mrs Edwards chuckled again.

'That's just what Mr Simon used to say when he was a teenager,' she confided, leading Holly back to the kitchen. 'He used to call it the morgue and he had some awful bad fights with his mama when he wanted to bring an electric guitar into his bedroom upstairs. Now, Miz Madigan, God rest her soul, she came from a real old family and she was dead set on doing everything by tradition. She couldn't imagine what she'd done to deserve such a hell-raiser for a son.'

Holly blinked, absorbing this fascinating and unlikely information about Simon Madigan's past. That his mother was dead, that they had clashed, that Simon was...

'A hell-raiser?' she echoed in disbelief.

Mrs Edwards suddenly seemed to realise that she had been gossiping about her employer. Her cheeks went pink, her lips pressed together and she hurried over to a far corner of the kitchen, where she began hauling china out of a cupboard and setting it on a tray.

'Well, he settled down just fine once he was grown,' she said over her shoulder. 'There ain't a smarter businessman in New Orleans, even if he don't seem as happy as...'

She left the sentence unfinished and Holly prudently busied herself with the preparations for cooking the wild rice. Yet once that was simmering safely on the stove and the ducks were basted with vermouth, she did indulge her curiosity by asking about the guests.

'Is this a business dinner tonight?' she asked. 'Or just for friends? I mean, will I need to clear the table quickly so they can put documents out on it or——'

Mrs Edwards sighed.

'No-o,' she said. 'It ain't officially a business dinner, but it ain't really for friends neither. Mr Simon don't bother much with friends, he's always too busy. Work, work, work, that's all that man ever does! Fifteen, sixteen hours a day. Like he's got some demon inside him drivin' him on. Even these people that are coming here tonight are all folks he knows through his business dealings. Jazz musicians, patents lawyers, accountants, sound engineers, photographers. No wife or steady girlfriend, not for him. Oh, no. You see, there are always women after him, but it never lasts. Either they get sick of being neglected for his work or he loses interest in them. The trouble is, he treats them like he treats his company takeovers. He always gets what he wants and then he doesn't want it any more. It's all just a game to him. But if he doesn't watch out, he's going to wind up the richest, busiest man in New Orleans and the loneliest. Now, according to him, this is a social evening, but I'll bet my last dime they wind up discussing album covers or some other foolishness before the dinner's over. But don't you worry none about that, honey. Your job's to get that meal on the table on time and nothing else.'

The housekeeper accompanied this last remark with a significant glance at the wooden station clock on the wall, which reminded Holly that time was slipping by. Although she was dying to ask just how Virginia Cox fitted into Simon's network of business associates, she turned her attention to the more pressing problem of what vegetables to cook. Green runner beans seemed like a safe choice and she soon had her hands plunged into a sinkful of chilled water. She was still paring off strings and trimming the ends when she heard the first car outside followed by the musical chime of the front doorbell.

'I hope Bob's all dressed in his dinner outfit and ready to act as barman,' worried Mrs Edwards aloud and crept out to check on her husband.

Left alone, Holly was free to let her thoughts drift for a while. The familiar routine of cooking had restored her shaken self-confidence and as the kitchen filled with the delicious aromas of duck and wild rice, she found her mind turning like a compass needle to Simon Madigan. His image flashed before her again as she had first seen him. The immaculate pale grey suit with the white shirt and striped tie seemed totally at odds with the wild man inside them. He was too fierce, too earthy, too primitive to be confined by such restraints. She saw again his powerful, upraised fists beating on the door, the scowling black eyebrows, the long creases in his cheeks and the tough, determined mouth. A shiver went through her. Simon Madigan reminded her of those menacing children's fairy-tales, with the wolf dressed up as a deceptively harmless sheep. Somehow she couldn't rid herself of the certainty that there was a raw, violent, untamed power that lurked beneath his urbane exterior and would one day break out. The idea both frightened and fascinated her. What would it be like to be in his arms and have those narrowed blue eyes searing you not with anger, but with passion? A little shiver went through her and she straightened her chef's hat, brushed down her white overall and turned back to the stove.

What was the matter with her? She didn't normally get involved with customers. Of course, she didn't even see them normally. While Heather had been catering for several years, Holly had been strictly a hotel and restaurant chef. Her world was the steamy, frantic, stainless steel back-stage section of the luxury hotels. She rarely caught a glimpse of the thick carpets or starched tablecloths of the dining-rooms. In most cases she never even saw the wealthy people who lingered amid the music and flowers and soft lights, consuming the delectable dishes she concocted. And now that her world had so suddenly and violently collided with theirs, she wasn't at all sure that she liked the experience. Being whisked into Simon

Madigan's home and seeing where he ate his meals and entertained his guests made her feel as uncomfortable as if she were a spy. And she felt doubly uncomfortable because she couldn't deny that she was very powerfully attracted to him. Which was another thing that baffled her. Ever since she had broken up with Dennis Clancy a year before, nobody had attracted her. And even Dennis had never made her feel such breathless, fluttering uncertainty every time he looked at her. Damn Simon Madigan! The sooner she was out of here, the better.

'How's it going, honey?' Mrs Edwards came bustling through the swing door, bringing with her a brief wave of noise. Clinking glasses, laughter, the murmur of voices from the distant living-room. 'Mr Simon said he'd like to eat at eight on the dot.'

Holly swung into frenzied action. Setting the shrimp Creole on the gas to reheat, she put some sugar and vinegar in a pan to caramelise. Then she removed the duck from the oven, drained off the fat and began to make the sauce. Chicken stock, orange juice, grated orange rind, lemon juice, Curaçao. Curaçao! She had forgotten to ask Simon for it. She turned to enlist Mrs Edwards' help, but found that the housekeeper had vanished again.

'Damn! I'll have to go and ask him myself.'

The last thing she wanted to do was confront Simon again, but there was no choice. Dragging off her white chef's hat and overall, she gave her curls a hasty pat, darted back to switch off the gas and made her way into the hall. This part of the house was unfamiliar to her and she spared a swift, admiring glance for the free flying staircase which spiralled up to the floor above. But she knew there was no time to waste. The sound of voices led her past some more gold-framed family portraits, a grandfather clock and a carved colonial sofa to the living-room door. For a moment she stood on the threshold, hoping to catch Simon's attention unobtrusively.

'Looks as if you have a visitor, Simon,' boomed a deep, friendly voice.

Holly's searching gaze located Simon in the centre of the room. He had changed out of his grey business suit and was wearing an even more formal black dinner suit with a white shirt and black tie. The grey-bearded man who had just spoken was holding his shoulder and directing his gaze to the door. And on the other side of him stood Virginia Cox, her lips still parted and one hand laid earnestly on Simon's arm, as if she were in the middle of arguing a point with him.

'Can I help you, Miss Thomson?'

His voice wasn't exactly hostile, but it wasn't particularly friendly, either. The deep, hoarse burr held a wary note, as if he thought Holly had come to announce some new disaster. She flashed him a swift, apologetic smile, but also felt a spurt of annoyance at the way he obviously expected trouble.

'The Curaçao?' she reminded him.

The faint furrow between his black eyebrows vanished. He almost smiled at her.

'Of course. Bob, get the lady a bottle of Curaçao from behind the bar, will you?'

The brief lull in the conversation ended and the voices buzzed around her more loudly than ever. After one swift, searching glance at Holly's face Simon took the bottle from the barman, handed it across to her and then turned back to his guests. With the exception of the grey-bearded man, who wore a simple plaid shirt and denim trousers, they all looked rich, glossy, successful. Right out of Holly's orbit. Not the kind of people she normally knew or even wanted to know. And yet now, for some absurd reason, she felt humiliated by Simon's casual dismissal. As she walked to the door, she tried hard to argue with herself. Don't be a fool! she thought savagely. What did you expect? That he'd offer you a drink and try to draw you into the conversation? You're here to work, not to socialise! But it didn't help. As she reached the door she glanced over her shoulder. Virginia gave her a bored, dismissive look and continued haranguing Simon. There was nothing exactly flirtatious in the woman's manner and her conversation didn't seem breathlessly romantic. As a matter of fact, she was talking very fast and very emphatically about pie charts and sales figures. Yet something in the way the two of them were behaving sent an odd pang of misgiving through Holly. Simon's head was lowered and he was listening to Virginia with an attentive frown, while she kept grasping his arm and gesturing as she made each point. Almost as if she owned him, thought Holly with distaste, and pressed her lips together in disapproval. Suddenly she realised that the man with the grey beard was watching her with quiet amusement. Her cheeks burned and, muttering something incoherent, she fled to the kitchen.

Fortunately she hadn't time to sit brooding like Cinderella, but had to tackle the sauce, which was beginning to cool. Years of training had made her adept at cooking even when her mind was on something else and at eight o'clock precisely she was able to announce that dinner was ready.

The first course was a huge success. The shrimp Creole was hot, spicy and thick with tomato and seafood so that enthusiastic compliments filled the room. And the duck with orange sauce, wild rice, creamed mushrooms and barely tender green beans met with similar approval. As she came back to remove the dirty plates after the main course, Holly felt a warm glow of achievement. When Simon Madigan lifted his wine glass in an approving toast and met her eyes without a trace of irony, she felt her triumph was complete.

'Nice going, Miss Thomson! We're all agreed that you're a great cook.'

She flushed and smiled back at him.

'Thank you, Mr Madigan,' she replied demurely. And then wondered why she had to smirk and simper like an idiot just because he offered her some well-earned praise.

Of course it was too good to last. She should have known that. All evening she had been dogged by the fear that something would go wrong and, as she was serving the final course, it did. In a corner of the dining-room, nestling snugly against the avocado-green walls, was a small mahogany table which Holly had draped with a white cloth. A few decorative heatproof mats and a spirit lamp had turned it into a handy serving station so that she didn't need to make a long trek to the kitchen for every plate and bowl. Setting the three cheesecakes down here, she cut them deftly into neat portions and slid them on to small plates. With two of these in her hands she walked across to the dining table, intending to put them in front of the guests. But by now, as Letty Edwards had predicted, the dinner was beginning to deteriorate. Large colour photos of rock album covers were being passed down the far side of the table and Virginia Cox was unfolding a long computer printout. A noisy argument appeared to be in progress.

'Excuse me,' murmured Holly, stretching forward with one of the plates.

But at that moment Virginia flapped her arms vigorously to unfold the document and disaster struck.

'Careful!' warned Holly. Too late!

Virginia struck her hand, the plate went flying and there was a sound of shattering crockery and glass.

'You clumsy fool!' shrieked Virginia.

Holly stared in horror. For one small plate, it had certainly done the maximum possible damage. First it had bounced against Virginia's chest, leaving an avalanche of cream cheese and butter pecan sauce down the front of her silver evening dress. Then it had ricocheted on to her wine glass, shattering both itself and the glass with the impact. And finally it had come to rest in a dozen spiky fragments all over the tablecloth, splattering everything in sight with red wine and cheese.

'Why did you ever employ this girl?' she demanded accusingly, turning to Simon. 'She's totally incompetent and should never have been let loose in a civilised household!'

'Now just a moment, Virginia——' began Simon protestingly, but Holly interrupted. She didn't need anyone else to fight her battles for her. There had been several occasions in her parents' restaurant when she had had to deal with abusive drunks. Virginia wasn't drunk, but she was certainly abusive, and Holly knew that it was important to calm her down before she really launched a scene.

'I'm sorry about what happened, Miss Cox,' she said soothingly. 'All over your beautiful dress, too! Here, won't you take this napkin and wipe it down while I pick up the pieces?'

She had a small plastic bin hidden under her serving table for just such an emergency, and now she whisked it out and hastily gathered up the broken fragments of cutlery and glass. While Virginia was still on her feet, swearing and muttering as she mopped her dress dry, Holly spread a couple of clean white linen napkins over the worst of the stains on the tablecloth, brushed off Virginia's chair, and begged her to sit down.

'I'm afraid I haven't any more cheesecake to offer you,' she explained. 'But I can make you some flambéed crêpes with Curaçao, if you like.'

'I hate crêpes,' snapped Virginia.

'Then take my cheesecake,' ordered Simon. 'And I'll be glad to eat the crêpes. Thank you, Miss Thomson.'

Holly shot him a brief grimace that was almost a smile and retreated into the kitchen. It disconcerted her a little to find him being so polite. Just when she had decided he was ruthless and unfeeling, he took her completely by surprise! On the whole she preferred the way he had behaved in the restaurant earlier in the day. It was simpler to dislike him outright than to feel this sneaking, hesitant gratitude towards him. But fortunately she had little time to brood on the matter.

Two minutes later she was back with a portable gas ring and a copper crêpe pan, along with the bottle of Curaçao. With unsteady fingers she lit the gas, bubbled some butter in the pan, and poured in the hastily prepared crêpe mixture. And expert flip with the spatula, a quick dash of Curaçao and a lighted match, and the whole thing went up in spectacular blue flames. There were gasps of admiration, and for the first time Holly began to feel that most of the people within the room were actually on her side. As the flames flickered and then died out, she slid the finished crêpe onto a plate and set it in front of Simon.

'I hope you enjoy it, sir,' she said, picking up her equipment and backing away.

When she reached the safety of the kitchen, Mrs Edwards looked up at her with interest from the breakfast-bar.

'What in the world happened in there?' she demanded.

With a grimace Holly told her.

'Oh, shoot! Don't you take no notice of her, honey,' advised the housekeeper. 'She acts the same way around me. Anyone that ain't rich or real smart she just despises and that's the truth.'

Holly smiled at her gratefully as she began preparing the coffee, but a dragging sense of failure oppressed her, as she weighed out the fragrant ground coffee and measured the water in the percolator. She had tried so hard and yet she had wrecked everything. It just wasn't fair! Glancing across at the housekeeper, she saw Mrs

Edwards give a jaw-cracking yawn as she peered at the crossword puzzle in front of her.

'Why don't you go to bed, Mrs Edwards? You can trust me to clean up the kitchen when I'm finished.'

'I'd love to, honey, but I can't,' confided Mrs Edwards. 'You see, Miss Cox is a house guest here, and some nights she likes to have this herbal tea stuff she calls tisane. I don't know if she'll want it tonight. Probably not after such a big dinner, but she might. So I have to stay up till she goes to bed, just to be sure.'

'That's simple enough,' said Holly. 'I'd be glad to make it for you. Although the way things are going tonight, I'm not even sure I can be trusted to pour boiling water into a teapot successfully.'

The housekeeper smiled.

'Well, I'd be real grateful if you would,' she admitted, rising to her feet.

The coffee was served without incident. Then the guests retired into the living-room, giving Holly a chance to clear up. The breakage of the Wedgwood plate and crystal wine glass still upset her, but there was nothing she could do except wrap the fragments in newspaper and throw them in the rubbish. After that she squirted the tablecloth with soda water to stop the stain from setting, and began the lengthy task of rinsing the plates and loading the dishwasher. In the distance she heard someone begin to play a saxophone and after a while it began to sound as if a full scale party was taking place in the living-room.

Holly sighed impatiently. By now her feet were aching, her temper was in shreds and she was longing to go home. Unfortunately, without a car of her own, she was entirely dependent on Simon Madigan to get her there. And she certainly couldn't leave until all this mess was brought under control. Doggedly she set to work, loading as much as she could into the dishwasher, and washing the rest by hand. After a while she heard the slam of car doors and the rattle of tyres on the gravel, but she was surprised when she glanced up at the clock on the wall and saw that it was after midnight. She was even more surprised when Simon Madigan suddenly came through the swing door of the dining-room.

Her back was turned and only the faint swish of the door and an odd, tingling sensation in her spine made her aware that she was no longer alone. Feeling absurdly nervous and keyed-up, she swivelled to face him. He was still wearing his black dinner trousers and pintucked white shirt, but he had discarded the jacket and tie and unbuttoned the collar. Her eyes were drawn irresistibly to the base of his throat where a tantalising glimpse of tanned, muscular chest was clearly visible. Holly glanced hastily away and felt her cheeks burn. But Simon had intercepted her gaze. And he continued to stare thoughtfully at her, as if he were working out what it meant.

'I apologise for my clothes,' he said in his deep, husky burr. 'Or lack of them. Virginia wasn't the only one to suffer from the cream cheese! I've put my jacket and tie in the dry-cleaning basket, but of course I'll change before I drive you home. I just wanted to come and pay you first.'

But Holly made no move to take the envelope which Simon held out to her. His glinting, blue-eyed appraisal was making her feel intensely shaken and uncomfortable. She had hoped that this moment would be one of triumph for her, a moment when she could wipe out the memory of her earlier clumsiness with the Curaçao bottle outside the restaurant. Instead the dinner had turned out to be a disaster and she was blushing and squirming like a teenage schoolgirl. It made her feel furious with herself. And with him. She darted another furtive glance at him and looked hastily away.

'Look, I'm... really sorry about what happened,' she said disjointedly. 'I should have checked more carefully before I served the cake. But naturally I'll replace the plate and glass if you can tell me where to buy——'

'Don't worry about it,' Simon cut in with an indifferent shrug. 'I doubt if you could match them anyway. They were over eighty years old.'

Holly felt worse than ever on learning that.

'Oh, no!' she groaned. 'Family heirlooms? That's terrible! Well, in that case, I certainly won't take any money from you for the dinner. Anyway that was our agreement, wasn't it? I offered you a money-back guarantee if you weren't satisfied.'

'Oh, but I am satisfied,' retorted Simon, watching her from beneath half closed lids. 'Satisfied and intrigued.'

'Intrigued?'

Alarm bells went off inside her brain. She didn't like the way that Simon was tilting his head to one side and scrutinising her as if she were an electric guitar up for sale. A thoughtful frown sharpened his features and he stood with his arms folded, apparently not caring about Holly's growing discomfiture. The cream envelope dangled negligently between two of his fingers like a weapon ready for use. And all the time the tension between them was building like the prelude to a violent storm.

'Yes. Intrigued,' he repeated in that hoarse drawl that sent little thrills of excitement chasing over her skin. 'But never mind that. What counts at the moment is that I owe you money and I want to pay it.'

'No, you don't!' gabbled Holly in a high, unnatural voice. 'You needn't pay me anything.'

It was not just the broken plate or the ruined meal. In some obscure way the envelope full of money that he was holding out to her seemed to be linked in her mind with the strange, physical effects that his presence was having on her. The dryness in her throat, the weakness in her knees, the sensual, fluttering warmth that was uncoiling deep inside her. She didn't want to be paid for these sensations. She didn't even want to have them! Horrified, she swung away and began frantically cramming a herbal teabag into a pot. Anything to keep her shaking fingers occupied.

'Look at me when I'm talking to you!' Simon thundered, crossing the room in two strides and shaking her arm. 'Damn you, you're being ridiculous! What are you doing there anyway?'

'M-making a herbal tisane for Miss Cox.'

'She won't need it. She's already gone upstairs to bed. Now stop that foolishness and tell me what's going on here. Why won't you accept my money?'

It had been a mistake to turn away from him, Holly realised that. For now that he was holding her arm and looking down at her with his blue eyes smouldering like smoky quartz, he seemed more dangerous than ever. And not only that. He was so close to her that she could feel the heat of his body radiating out to meet her and sense the muscular tension in those powerful, masculine thighs. With a sudden low growl of impatience, he tossed the envelope on the counter and seized her by the shoulders.

'Why won't you accept my money?' he said through his teeth.

He was so close he could have kissed her and the thought of that made her feel faint with desire. Every nerve in her body was screaming a primal response to his warmth, his strength, his nearness. She caught her breath, agonisingly aware of the spicy masculine scent of his body, the hard, insistent pressure of his hands, the way his muscular legs were planted wide apart. As if he were going to engulf me, she thought. A shameful thrill of excitement went through her at the image and she gasped softly.

'Well?' he insisted. 'Why won't you?'

Suddenly she found her voice. She couldn't stand here all night behaving as if she were half-witted. He was entitled to some sort of answer, even if she felt just as bewildered as he did at the way she was acting.

'B-because you said everything had to be perfect. And it wasn't. I messed it up.'

He gave an exasperated growl of laughter.

'Don't be a fool. It was damned near perfect. The food was wonderful.'

'But I dropped the cheesecake, I broke the plate, I upset one of your guests.'

His face was suddenly so fierce that it made her quail. With an inner pang she realised how annoyed he must be. But his next words surprised her.

'That was a genuine accident,' he snapped. 'And it's not you I blame for it. Virginia bumped your arm, we all saw it. Perhaps she couldn't help that, but she had no need to speak to you the way she did. If she were my wife, I would insist that she apologise to you. Since she's only my guest, I can hardly compel her, but you certainly have my apologies for any humiliation you suffered.'

'Thank you,' said Holly shakily.

'You're welcome,' replied Simon. And then added unwisely, 'I hate to see people being rude to the hired help. Now take your money like a good girl and stop being absurd!'

He reached past her to pick up the envelope again, but somehow his patronising tone touched Holly on the raw. Damn him, she didn't want his money! All she wanted was to be out of here.

'No!' she cried in a stifled voice.

With a growl of exasperation he seized her hands and tried to thrust the envelope into them, but she clenched her fists and pushed him away. For a moment they struggled and Holly heard her breath coming in deep, uneven gulps. She knew her whole attitude was crazy, but she couldn't stop it. The words 'hired help' echoed in her head and a surge of fury went through her. She didn't want Simon Madigan to see her only as the 'hired help', she wanted him to...to what? Her amber-coloured eyes flicked up in alarm to meet his and she gave a soft whimper deep in her throat. For in that moment she knew exactly how she wanted Simon to see her. As a woman, full of needs and yearnings and pride, just like his own. The sudden tension in her muscles, the quiver of longing and dismay that went through her seemed to communicate some secret message to Simon. His dark blue eyes narrowed, his nostrils flared and his lips parted. Holly felt rather than saw how his whole body suddenly tensed and paused like a leopard's about to spring. Then he caught his breath, flung the envelope away and hauled her against him in a savage embrace.

Holly had never been kissed so brutally in her life. And yet as she felt herself arched back against the counter, as her hair fell in disorder, her eyes closed and a dizzy, pulsating warmth spread through every cell of her body, she knew that she wanted this more than anything in her entire life. Simon's hands were threaded ruthlessly through her hair, his lips quivered on hers and his massive, virile body crushed against hers with an urgency that terrified and elated her. He growled a hoarse endearment and buried his face in her throat, inhaling her perfume and leaving a trail of brief, unsatisfying kisses on her skin. A shudder of sheer delight went through her and she shifted sensually, not even caring when she heard the clatter of an overturning cup behind her. All she cared about now was the heady intoxication of Simon's caresses, the rasp of his chin against her smooth throat, the torment of his skilful, maddening hands moving in spirals down her back. And then there was that faint swish again, an odd, tingling sensation that had nothing to do with Simon's touch. With a gasp of dismay, Holly tried to struggle free, but it was too late. As she had feared, they were no longer alone.

'My dear Simon,' said Virginia in a tone of mingled contempt and amusement. 'If you must seduce the servants, do you have to do it where you'll destroy my supper tray?'

CHAPTER THREE

IT WAS probably the most humiliating moment of Holly's life. Virginia was standing just inside the kitchen door with a contemptuous half-smile on her face. She was dressed in an elegantly cut, navy blue satin dressing-gown and the soft leather bedroom slippers which had enabled her to enter the room so quietly. If she had an ounce of tact, thought Holly, she would have crept out as quietly as she came in! But obviously that wasn't Virginia's intention at all. And with a flash of unhappy insight, Holly realised why. She's still furious with me about the cheesecake, she thought. She wants to embarrass me as much as she possibly can.

'Well, Simon,' purred Virginia. 'Would you like me to leave?'

At Virginia's first words, Simon had swung round and backed himself against the counter so that he was shoulder to shoulder with Holly. For an instant, his arm had remained tightened around her shoulders, then he abruptly released her. Now she glanced sideways at him, desperately hoping to catch his eye. But he seemed equally unmoved either by her confusion or by Virginia's scornful amusement. His features remained completely calm and impassive, except for a faint ironic twist to the corners of his mouth.

'That might be tactful,' he agreed.

Virginia gave a mirthless laugh.

'I see,' she said sweetly. 'Then as soon as I've had my tisane, I'll tactfully leave.'

And to Holly's amazement, she came straight over to them, seized the tray and set the overturned cup upright upon it. Holly waited in horror for Simon to make some protest, to put an end to this ridiculous and impossible scene. But all he did was to pull her out of Virginia's way with a careless gesture, as if none of it really mattered very much. Holly's embarrassment suddenly gave way to a boiling anger. How dared Simon allow her to flounder in such a humiliating situation? Stalking across the room, she picked up her handbag, and stood decisively by the back door.

'I'm the one who should leave,' she announced. 'Will you please give me a lift home now, Mr Madigan?'

Simon shrugged. His sardonic smile grew more pronounced, and his dark blue eyes drifted lazily from Virginia to Holly, as if he was enjoying the byplay between them.

'Sure, if you want me to,' he agreed. 'But I'll go up and change first.'

'Please don't bother,' snapped Holly. 'The sooner I get out of here, the better.'

Fifteen minutes later they were driving along the road beside the tranquil, moonlit river. Out on the water a paddlesteamer glided silently along, its shape outlined by brightly coloured lights. Dark shapes of trees clustered on the opposite bank and there was no sound but the hiss of the tyres and the purr of the car's airconditioning. The scene could hardly have been more tranquil, and yet Holly felt anything but tranquil. Her initial embarrassment and anger had given way to a chill feeling of disbelief. Mile after mile passed and Simon continued to say nothing. From time to time he glanced at her, but the glances didn't seem either embarrassed or pleading. Instead they were keen, scrutinising, leisurely, as if he were sizing her up. He made her feel furious and perplexed. Why doesn't he say something? she thought angrily, and yet when he did finally speak it came as a complete surprise to her.

'I'm sorry about that stupid little incident in the kitchen, Heather,' he announced in a matter of fact voice.

Stupid little...! What did he mean? That kissing her was foolish and insignificant? She was so taken aback that she stammered the first thing that came to her head.

'I'm not Heather.'

'*What*?'

At least that got a reaction. His startled gaze flew to her face and the car swerved briefly before recovering.

'Oh, don't look at me as if I've gone off my head!' exclaimed Holly crossly. 'Heather had an accident three weeks ago and went into hospital for an emergency operation.'

Simon whistled softly.

'Then who in the name of all that's wonderful are you?'

'Her sister. My name's Holly. I flew over from Hawaii to help out as soon as I knew she was injured.'

'Is she all right now?'

The concern in his voice was so apparent that Holly thawed slightly towards him.

'Not quite, but she's getting better,' she admitted grudgingly. 'Her leg is in traction and she had quite a bad bump on her head. I suppose that's why she forgot to tell me about your dinner booking.'

'You mean you didn't know about it?'

'Not until you showed up at the restaurant this afternoon.'

'So you put on an unscheduled dinner for thirty people at two hours' notice?' said Simon wonderingly.

'Yes,' she replied with a touch of pride.

'Hmm. Impressive. So you're not the incompetent scatterbrain that I first thought.'

'No, I'm not!'

The antagonism in her voice was unmistakable. It vibrated around the tiny interior of the car. And even in the moonlight she was aware of Simon glancing sideways at her grimly set chin and scowling features. He gave a low growl of laughter, and there was a note of admiration in his voice when he spoke again.

'You're quite a woman... Holly. Especially when you're being kissed.'

'Don't!' she choked indignantly.

'Why not?' he demanded. 'I enjoyed it and I had the impression that you did, too. It was the best part of the evening.'

Even now, after the way he had behaved, that smouldering baritone still sent treacherous flares of desire darting through her veins. She took in breath in a long, dragging gulp and tried not to listen.

'Why did you kiss me anyway?' she blurted out.

'Because I wanted to. What's the problem? Are you having second thoughts about it?'

'It should never have happened,' she cried.

Simon's eyebrows rose.

'Why not?' he demanded.

'Because I was there as a professional chef, not as a—not as a——' she left the sentence unfinished. 'I don't know about you, Mr Madigan, but I don't kiss people I don't know. All I want to do is forget that the whole thing ever happened!'

He tilted his head on one side for a moment as if he were thinking, then abruptly he shrugged.

'Just as you like,' he agreed coolly.

The ease with which he dismissed the episode made Holly feel worse than ever. It was one thing for her to say she wanted to forget it, but how could she? And Simon's willingness to brush it off so easily made her realise that it had meant nothing to him, nothing at all. To her dismay she realised that she wanted him to protest, to argue with her, to insist that he must see her again. Instead he simply gazed at the moonlit road ahead of them, with a faint, almost bored smile playing around his lips. Biting her lip, she stared out of the side window of the car into the darkness, until at last the lights of the city began to approach. She gave him the address of her sister's apartment and was furious to hear a tremor in her voice. But even then the ordeal was not over.

It was after one a.m. when the car drew up beside the kerb in front of the old terraced house where Heather's apartment was located. Even at this late hour there was still plenty going on in the street. It must have rained some time during the evening and the road was dark and shiny with moisture. All along the pumpkin-coloured stucco façade of the building, ornate wrought-iron lamps cast welcoming pools of light on the pavement below. Most of the long green shutters were closed, but here and there light showed where a party was still in progress. Groups of people returning home from late-night revels sauntered along the pavements, and a horse-drawn surrey trotted briskly by. On the street corner a black saxophone player was playing some mournful jazz.

'I'll see you up to your apartment,' offered Simon.

'There's no need,' insisted Holly. 'You can see there are plenty of people about. I'll be fine.'

'You've forgotten about all that equipment you have to carry,' he pointed out.

'I'll manage!' retorted Holly.

With a faint snort of derision, he climbed out of the car, opened the boot and took one large carton under each arm. Without another word he headed for the front door of the house, so that Holly was left to close the boot and scurry after him.

'Where is it?' he demanded over his shoulder.

'Second floor. On the left,' she replied.

Smouldering with annoyance, she fumbled in her bag and produced a key. It was a pity her niece Amber was sleeping over at the neighbour's apartment tonight, or she would have had the babysitter as an ally. As it was, she showed Simon through the front door with the barest minimum of courtesy. Snapping on the light in the living-room, she gestured to the kitchen, which lay beyond.

'Just put them on the table, if you would, please,' she instructed.

If he expected coffee, he was in for a disappointment. As far as Holly was concerned, there was nothing on offer for him, now, or ever again. He dumped the cartons and returned to the tiny front hall, where she stood waiting with the front door still open. He smiled sardonically.

'What's the matter?' he taunted. 'Getting ready to scream if the going gets tough?'

'If you say so,' she replied coldly.

'Don't be a fool, Holly,' he snapped.

And before she could protest, he had dragged her inside the front door and slammed it shut. Then with a swift movement, he flattened his palms against its wood, trapping her between his arms. The blue eyes glinted down at her in the faint light of the hall.

'Stop play-acting. You know you have nothing to fear from me. Listen, why don't we go to a nightclub on Saturday? Pat O'Brien's has a terrific floorshow.'

'No! Anyway I'm working Saturday.'

'Then when can I see you again?'

'Never,' croaked Holly.

For a moment longer he stood looking down at her, observing the way her breasts heaved under the dark material of her dress, and clearly amused by the panic in her eyes. Then he released her and opened the door. His lips twisted mockingly.

'Never is a long time,' he reminded her.

Then he was gone.

Holly was woken from a restless, confusing sleep by the insistent shrilling of the doorbell. Blinking and shuddering, she groped her way into a thin cotton dressing-gown and went to open the front door. It was Simon, clutching a huge bouquet of yellow roses. He leaned negligently against the doorframe and his eyes lit up at the sight of Holly. Thrusting the bouquet at her, he gave her a lazy smile.

'How about lunch?' he drawled. 'We could go to the Top of the Mart restaurant. It's got a great view of the city.'

'No, thank you.'

Holly's voice was clipped, brittle, dismissive. The scent of roses filled the air and for an instant she was tempted to bury her face in those moist, delicate petals. Then she stepped back a pace, hastily putting her hands behind her back. She didn't want Simon's flowers. Or him. She wanted nothing further to do with him.

'What's the matter?' he asked in a hurt voice. 'Don't you like roses?'

The plaintive tone infuriated her. She was damned sure he was putting it on! And yet for a moment she thought she saw a genuine flare of disappointment in his eyes. She hesitated, biting her lip.

'It's not that. I don't think you should give me flowers. I——'

'Well, give them to your sister, then,' he urged. 'Maybe they'll cheer her up.'

Put that way, it was impossible to refuse. Eyeing him dubiously, Holly reached out and took the flowers. An unmistakable glint of triumph flashed in Simon's eyes.

'You manipulative swine,' she breathed.

He didn't deny it. A faint, mocking smile twisted the corners of his mouth and he returned her gaze with a frank, admiring appraisal. Tension flared between them like voltage travelling along a wire.

'How about lunch?' he repeated.

'No!'

She was suddenly conscious of the steamy heat in the hallway, of the overpowering fragrance of roses that was making her head swim. And, worse still, of some other nameless and far more potent force that was making her heart race and her breath come in shallow, fluttering gulps.

'Why not?'

'I'm busy. And I don't want to have lunch with you.'

Her voice was bitter, suspicious, charged with resentment at the way he had already humiliated her. Yet her antagonism seemed to pass him by, leaving him blithely unaware of it.

'Are you sure? I cancelled an important meeting so I could take you out.'

Now that really infuriated her. What was she supposed to do? Fall on her knees and kiss his feet in gratitude? Her tawny eyes flashed dangerously.

'You amaze me,' she said drily. 'But the answer is still no.'

She expected him to argue and almost relished the thought of a knock-down, drag-out fight with him. Instead he simply gave a careless shrug, raised one hand in a casual farewell and backed out of the doorway. Holly felt an absurd pang of disappointment.

'Suit yourself. Maybe some other time then. I'll call you tomorrow.'

'No!'

She rushed out on to the landing after him, but he was already vanishing down the stairwell with swift, purposeful steps as if he had more important matters to tackle.

'Simon! I won't go with you! Do you hear me? I won't!'

Her voice echoed through the building and his amused baritone floated back up in response, serene and untroubled.

'Fine, Holly. Whatever you like.'

'Mmmph! Damn him!' cried Holly, venting her rage by slamming the front door as she retreated inside. All she had achieved was to make herself feel intensely foolish. And she wasn't even sure that she had succeeded in driving him away. Would he heed her warning or not?

Half an hour later it seemed she had her answer when the doorbell rang again. Simon Madigan! she thought, and felt instantly ashamed at the way her pulses raced. But this time it wasn't Simon. Standing on the doormat was Heather's next-door neighbour Betty Mae Cooper, with two little girls held firmly by the hand. Both were jigging up and down with excitement and Holly's appearance was greeted with squeals of joy.

'Aunt Holly, Mrs Cooper is going to take Jessie and me to the zoo if you say I can go. Please, please can I?'

Holly smiled down at the two eager faces, one so dark and the other so fair.

'I don't know, Amber,' she said. 'I was going to take you to visit Mommy at the hospital today.'

'Don't worry about it,' said Betty Mae. 'I'll take her into the hospital on the way back from the zoo. She can still see her Mommy.'

'That's awfully kind of you,' exclaimed Holly, thinking what wonderful neighbours Heather had. 'All right then, I can hardly refuse. But have you got time for a cup of coffee before you leave?'

The other woman rolled her eyes comically.

'I don't think so, honey. I think all we have time for is to catch the first streetcar to the zoo. Right, girls?'

'Right!' squealed both little girls in chorus.

Still smiling to herself, Holly said goodbye and paused to listen for a moment as their skipping footsteps and shrill voices echoed down the stairwell. Then she closed the front door and leaned against it. With a sigh, she ran her fingers through her tumbled ginger hair. In some ways, she almost regretted allowing Amber to go. With a boisterous five-year-old to keep occupied all day, she would have had no time to brood over her own problems. But now there was no excuse. She must decide what she was going to do about Simon Madigan. Padding her way into the kitchen on bare feet, she switched on the coffee percolator, and began fixing herself a fresh fruit salad. Yet even the sight of luscious fresh peaches, watermelon, cantaloupe wedges, lime juice and creamy yoghurt did little to raise her spirits. She had an uneasy feeling that Simon Madigan was not going to give up easily in his determination to see her again.

She didn't even bother to try and switch on the noisy air-conditioner that sat in the middle of the other window. She knew already that it didn't work, and there was no likelihood that it would be fixed any time soon. Any spare cash that Heather ever had was always spent on her daughter Amber or on the restaurant, not on comforts for the home. Well, as soon as she had finished eating, she would go and take a long, cool shower and then visit Heather in the hospital. That would give her something to do other than brood about Simon.

Unfortunately, the mere thought of his name acted like a starting gun, setting her unruly feelings into violent motion. Every detail of that disturbing evening flashed back to her. How he had erupted into the tiny restaurant, how he had treated her like a servant for most of the evening, and then how he had kissed her in the kitchen. She winced at the memory. It wasn't as though she had never been kissed before. After all, she was twenty-six years old, a grown woman. But kisses had always meant something to Holly, and she felt humiliatingly certain that those kisses last night had meant absolutely nothing to Simon Madigan. What did she know about him, after all? Only that he had an extraordinary physical magnetism and that he was far too fond of giving orders. And far too ready to amuse himself with any female who happened to be passing by.

Obviously, he was so arrogant that he only viewed women as the instruments of his pleasure, not as human beings with feelings. And why was a man of his age behaving so irresponsibly? After all, he must be thirty-four or thirty-five, so why wasn't he married? Why hadn't he made a commitment to some woman already? With his looks and wealth, dozens of women should have jumped at the chance to marry him! The fact that it hadn't happened must mean that there was something seriously wrong with his character. No doubt other women had figured out for themselves just how shallow and callous and exploitative he was! And why was he pursuing her now? Probably because her own impulsive and foolish behaviour the previous evening had made him think she was an easy conquest. Well, I'm certainly not going to get trapped in his net, thought Holly resentfully. If what he wants is meaningless sex, he can go elsewhere for it.

Even the cool shower didn't help her spirits much, and she was even more annoyed when she unpacked one of her cartons of equipment to discover that Simon had tucked the envelope full of money inside the rice steamer. She felt a strong urge to tear the banknotes up or fling them in the garbage, but cooler reflection prevailed. Heather needed that money and would have to be given it. All the same, by the time Holly set off to see her at the hospital, she was feeling thoroughly depressed. Yet she tried to remind herself how much more fortunate she was than her sister. Poor Heather! Lying there in traction in a hospital bed, with a mountain of problems waiting for her when she finally was well enough to come home. Although Heather never complained, Holly could guess shrewdly at some of the loneliness and heartache of being a single mother. Not only that, but there were the never-ending financial worries. The postman had come while she was in the shower and she had a dismal suspicion that most of the piles of letters for Heather were bills. Well, at least she could buy her some candy to cheer her up! Armed with Simon's yellow roses and a box of pralines, Holly finally stepped off the streetcar outside the hospital. Its welcome coolness enveloped her, and she rode up in the elevator to Heather's ward. It was a two-bedded room, but at the moment the other bed was empty, so Heather was the sole occupant. Holly grimaced at the sight of the leg hoisted up in the air, but went forward to kiss her sister. Heather sat up eagerly and then tried to hide her disappointment at the fact that Holly was alone.

'Didn't Amber want to come?' she asked in a forlorn voice.

Holly smiled.

'Relax. She's gone to the zoo with Betty Mae Cooper and Betty will bring her over later. Never mind about her, she's fine. But what did the doctor say about you? When do they think you'll be out of here?'

Heather's face shadowed.

'At least another four to six weeks,' she sighed. 'Will that be a problem for you, staying on here in New Orleans?'

Holly clicked her tongue.

'Don't be silly,' she exclaimed. 'I told you before, I'll stay as long as you like. I'm only concerned about you, Heather. I want you to get well as fast as you can.'

Not knowing what else to say, she thrust the flowers and the candy at her sister. Heather flashed her a rueful smile.

'I'm sorry,' she exclaimed. 'I didn't mean to sound ungrateful, but I'm just so worried about everything. Amber. The restaurant. All the bills. The repairs that the local government authority wants me to do. It's all too much for me.'

'Well, don't think about it,' advised Holly practically. 'Here's something more cheerful. I brought your mail in for you and I can see there's a letter from Mom and Dad.'

Heather opened it and scanned it, wrinkling her nose and smiling as she read.

'Mom wants me to bring Amber to Hawaii for a holiday as soon as I get out of hospital,' she confided. 'She's sent me the tickets.'

'Well, good. You should go. It'll help you recover.'

'But how can I afford to be off work for so long?' asked Heather anxiously.

'I'll help you. I'll stay as long as you like. Now what else have you got there? Any lottery prizes or inheritances from long-lost great aunts?'

Heather made a face.

'You wish! No. I think this one is from the local government authority and I have a rotten feeling that I'm not going to like what it says.'

Slowly and with a look of dread on her face, Heather ripped open the envelope, unfolded it and scanned the contents. Her cheeks went as white as paper and tears sprang to her eyes.

'What is it?' cried Holly. 'Let me see that! Oh, Heather. They can't mean it.'

'They do mean it!' insisted Heather shakily. 'It says so right here. If I don't get those repairs done to the restaurant within sixty days, they'll close me down. It'll be the end of everything I've worked for, Holly!'

Suddenly Heather's face crumpled and she snatched the letter off the bed and flung it savagely on the floor. Clicking her tongue, Holly scurried to retrieve it.

'Don't cry, Heather!' she begged. 'We'll find a way out of it.'

'How? If it were only the broken floor-tiles, it would be OK, but they say the plumbing in the men's bathroom has to be ripped out and replaced. There's no way I can afford that!'

'Takings have been good lately.'

'But not good enough. If only the outside catering part of the business would pick up a bit, maybe we could swing it. If I just had one or two more customers like Simon Madigan, I might have a fighting chance.'

Holly froze at the mention of that name. Her stomach seemed to lurch away from her and she felt the blood rush out of her face. Hastily she scrambled to her feet, hoping her sister hadn't noticed. Yet even in the midst of her misery, Heather was observant.

'What's wrong, Holly? You look as if you've seen a ghost.'

'Not a ghost. Simon Madigan,' muttered Holly.

'What? You saw him? When?'

With a reluctant sigh Holly gave her the barest possible outline of what had happened the previous evening, leaving out any mention of the fiasco in the kitchen. An incredulous smile of admiration and hope crept over Heather's features.

'Holly, that's wonderful!' she exclaimed. 'You're a miracle worker, you really are! Dinner for thirty at two hours' notice at Chartres House... I can't believe it. Three or four more functions like that and we could get the restaurant repairs done and be out of trouble. Mr Madigan is always really generous.'

'Yes, isn't he?' retorted Holly with an edge to her voice. She tossed the envelope full of banknotes on to the bed. 'Really generous! He just chases what he wants and pays for it.'

A puzzled frown knitted Heather's brows. She barely glanced at the money in the envelope before gazing searchingly at Holly.

'What happened?' she demanded. 'What did he do to make you so angry, Holly?'

Holly crossed to the window and gazed sombrely down at the street far below. For a moment she was tempted to keep her misery and turmoil to herself, but she and Heather had always been close. Besides her sister might worry more if she were kept in ignorance.

'He kissed me,' she said baldly. The words seemed to hurt her throat and she felt a small, stark smile pin itself to her lips. 'In the kitchen when I was washing up. He came in and kissed me.'

Heather was staring at her with as much horror as if Holly had just confessed that Simon had plunged a dagger into her heart.

'But why?' she protested. 'He's never been the kind of guy to feel up women who work for him. Besides, he wouldn't need to. He's always got hordes of beautiful, wealthy, high-powered females chasing after him. So what brought this on?'

'I don't know,' replied Holly huskily.

'Were you willing?'

'No. Yes. I don't know. I suppose so. Yes. Yes, I was. Then.'

'But not now?'

Holly turned back from the window, her eyes bright with unshed tears and a lump in her throat.

'Not if it's what I think it is.'

'And what do you think it is?'

'A pick-up. Another little frolic like good old Dennis's idea of a fun relationship.'

Holly's voice broke and she had to dig her nails savagely into her palms and blink rapidly before she could control herself. Heather, trapped on the bed, stretched out one hand to her.

'Oh, God, men are such bastards! Look at us, Holly. You and Dennis. Brian and me. All they want is one thing and the moment they've had it, they vanish.'

Holly squeezed Heather's hand and gave her a troubled smile. It wasn't the first time she had heard this complaint from her sister and who could blame her for feeling bitter? Ever since her boyfriend had abandoned her six years before, leaving her pregnant and broken-hearted, Heather had taken a very dim view of men. Unexpectedly Holly found herself springing to Simon's defence.

'I doubt if he's as bad as Brian was,' she said. 'After all, it was only a kiss.'

'So far,' sniffed Heather. 'But you ought to be careful, Holly. Simon's a good-looking man with a lot of charm. Maybe he'll start out with kisses, but it won't be long before he wants more. And you can bet your bootees he's not planning on marrying you.'

'How can you be so sure?' demanded Holly, feeling rather nettled by this.

'Oh, grow up, Holly! It'll be just like Dennis all over again. Rich, handsome, powerful men don't marry nobodies. They don't fall for women like us, they simply use us and abandon us. You know it's true.'

Holly was silent, feeling stabbed to the heart by her sister's words. And yet she couldn't deny the truth of what Heather was saying. Was it really likely that Simon had any plans for a serious relationship with her? Of course not!

'I suppose you're right,' she said with a sigh.

'Sure I am,' retorted Heather grimly. 'And you ought to be careful with Simon Madigan, Holly. Don't let your guard down for an instant.'

'I won't.'

'And another thing. If he asks you to do any more catering for him, you don't have to agree. I don't want you wrecking your happiness just to save my restaurant.'

'Don't worry,' replied Holly stormily. 'He'll probably never come near me again.'

'He will,' warned Heather. 'You can bet your life on that.'

CHAPTER FOUR

FOR the next week, it seemed as if Heather's prophecy was quite wrong. Holly's days fell into a predictable pattern. In the mornings she collected her niece Amber and often Mrs Cooper's little girl Jessie and took them both out on excursions. Visits to parks, rides on paddle steamers, excursions to museums and playgrounds. At three o'clock each afternoon she turned up at La Crevette, ready for the long night in the restaurant. From then on she was too frantically busy to think much about Simon Madigan. And when she came home at two or three in the morning she was too exhausted. But at odd moments, especially on the rare occasions when she found herself alone, a strange feeling of desolation would sweep through her. And, inexplicably, it was all linked with the thought of Simon Madigan. Why doesn't he phone me? she wondered one day, and hated herself for the thought. She didn't want him to phone, she told herself severely. She never wanted to see him again. Yet that didn't stop her heart from pounding like a triphammer the morning that she answered her doorbell and found him on the mat outside the door. If he had shown the slightest sign of wanting to kiss her or touch her, she probably would have slammed the door in his face. As it was, he simply stood there with his hands resting on his hips and a faint, bored smile on his face.

She caught her breath, taking in every detail of his dark, shiny hair, his lean, brooding features and his keen blue eyes. And yet, in spite of his nonchalant expression, his whole body exuded that same potent animal magnetism that had attracted her so powerfully on their first meeting. Perhaps he's unaware of it, she thought, stepping back a pace. Perhaps he really can't help it. Today he was less formally dressed than on the previous occasion. Beige drill trousers, a short-sleeved beige and blue checked shirt, a plaited tan belt that accentuated the narrowness of his hips, comfortable leather boat shoes. And yet mysteriously the whole effect was still one of power and authority. For the first time she noticed the coarse dark hairs on the backs of his arms, the powerful muscles under the suntanned skin and, for one crazy minute, wondered what the rest of his body would look like without any clothes. Then she saw how he was watching her from under half-lowered lids, and flushed scarlet.

'May I come in?' he asked lazily. 'I have some business to discuss with you.'

'Yes. Yes, of course.'

She waved him into the sitting-room. Without even waiting to be asked, he dropped into one of the shabby armchairs and leaned back, appraising her. It was Holly who sat nervously on the edge of her chair, tensed for flight, waiting for him to explain why he was there. And yet when he did, the explanation came almost as a disappointment.

'I thought you might do some more catering for me,' he announced bluntly.

'Oh. What did you have in mind?' she asked.

'I'm gearing up for a takeover bid on a small firm. I'll be doing a huge amount of work over the next week with my attorneys and accountants, so I want you to come in and provide lunch and dinner for us each day. And lots of coffee. That way we won't have to leave the building any more than is strictly necessary.'

Holly blinked.

'But the restaurant——' she stammered.

'You found a substitute once before. I'm sure you can again. And I'll pay you well.'

Holly thought of Heather and all the repairs that were needed at La Crevette. It was her duty, really, wasn't it? But did she have to feel such a shameful pang of excitement at the thought?

'Where would I have to serve these meals?' she asked, trying to cover her turmoil with a businesslike manner.

'In my office building. You may want to cook there too—I do have a small kitchen on the premises. If you're interested, I'll take you over there right now. But please tell me if you're not. I don't have a whole lot of time to waste.'

Holly flashed him a troubled look. If he didn't have a whole lot of time to waste, then why was he here making this offer in person? Why hadn't he simply asked a secretary to phone and arrange it? Surely he must be interested in Holly herself and not just the food she could produce. Mustn't he? But his impassive features gave nothing away. Only the drumming of his fingertips on his powerful thigh hinted at a certain impatience. With a conscious effort of will she dragged her gaze away from his hand and back to his face. She *must* remember that this was a business discussion. Strictly business.

'I'm interested,' she said crisply, rising to her feet. 'And I'd like to go and see the premises.'

Five minutes later, he stopped the car in the car park of a gleaming multi-storey building on the waterfront. In contrast to some of the decrepit-looking warehouses around it, this one was glossy and immaculately painted in attractive shades of silver and pale blue. Holly couldn't help being impressed by the vast lobby with its marble-tiled floors, masses of greenery and a reception desk made of solid mahogany. Simon led the way to the lift and pressed a button set in a brass panel.

'Which part of the building is your firm in?' asked Holly.

'All of it,' replied Simon.

She gaped.

'It must be huge,' she exclaimed. 'I didn't think a CD company could take up that much space!'

'I have other business interests too,' he said. 'Mainly in shipping. Cotton. Sugar cane. That sort of thing. And oil from the Gulf of Mexico.'

On the sixth floor, they stepped out into a reception area with apricot-coloured walls, deep, soft grey carpet, and a hushed atmosphere. A middle aged woman in a jade green suit immediately appeared from one of the offices and came to meet them. She was short, plump and efficient-looking with a pleasant, but determined expression.

'Holly, this is Joan Reynolds, my private secretary. Joan, Holly Thomson, who's likely to be doing the catering for us this week.'

'Hi. How are you?' said Joan with a smile. Then she turned to Simon. 'Mr Madigan, I've had five urgent phone calls for you while you were out. One from Frankfurt about the distribution problems with the cassettes in the Eastern bloc countries. And Bill Collins at Swanee Cotton wants you to call him back right away. The other three can wait a little longer, so I've left the messages on your desk.'

'Fine. Thank you, Joan. Will you take care of Holly for me and show her around?'

And with that he vanished into a large, light office overlooking the river. Left alone with the secretary, Holly found the other woman casting a swift, appraising glance over her simple green polo top and vivid Hawaiian printed skirt. Joan shook her head, as if baffled.

'I can't imagine why he had to go and pick you up himself,' she announced. 'He's so busy he hasn't got time to turn around right now. Not that he ever does.'

As she spoke, a mobile phone in a nearby office shrilled imperiously and she had to run and answer it. Another message for Simon. And so it continued during the next twenty minutes while she was showing Holly over the kitchen and boardroom areas and explaining the meal requirements.

'Is he always as busy as this?' asked Holly in disbelief, after Joan dealt with the eleventh phone call.

'Oh, yes, honey. Always. I worry that he'll work himself into the grave if he doesn't ease up.'

In the week that followed Holly began to have the same worry. For of course she took the job, as she had always known she would. She tried to tell herself that she had only accepted because the pay was so marvellous or because the hours left her free to play with Amber in the mornings and tuck her into bed at night. Yet deep down she knew that the main reason she had done it was for the bittersweet pleasure of being near Simon. So it infuriated her to find that most of the time Simon seemed to be wholly unaware of her presence.

At first she simply found it exasperating to see her delicate soufflés collapse, her veal escalopes grow cold and hard, her salads lose their crisp freshness while Simon drove a mid-morning meeting relentlessly through until three or even four o'clock. And it annoyed her to watch him shovelling down a delectable plateful of peeled shrimps and Mardi Gras rice with a pile of reports open in front of him, obviously without a clue as to what he was eating. Yet, after a while, her irritation began to change to alarm. It couldn't be good for him to work so hard, surely? At least the other men and women at these meetings seemed to go home sometimes, to make a few concessions to families and relaxation and a life outside the office. But Simon never stopped working. She began to suspect that he even slept in the office. If he ever slept.

On the last morning of her contract, Holly went to the office early. Very early. Amber had insisted on sleeping overnight at the neighbour's apartment with her little friend Jessie, so there was nothing to keep her at home. She told herself that she simply wanted to get a good start on the day, but she knew that wasn't the truth. What she was really hoping for was to find Simon alone. Not to flirt with him. No, not that. Just to be near him.

She did find him alone, but not in the way she had imagined. What she found was not the well-groomed, alert businessman. It was Simon as she had never seen him before. As she crept softly into the boardroom, she stopped dead. For Simon was sprawled in the grey leather recliner chair at the far end and he was fast asleep. His jacket was crumpled untidily on a side table with his tie snaked across it, his shirt was open at the throat and his head drooped to one side. With a soft exclamation of impatience, Holly tiptoed closer. He looked exhausted. Unshaven, rumpled, with dark shadows under his eyes. And yet even in that defenceless condition he was still alarmingly handsome. Relaxed in sleep, his mouth no longer had the taut, ironical set that it wore in his waking hours. Instead it smiled softly. And the way that he sighed and stirred, flexing his powerful arms and muttering, made him look heartachingly desirable. He was like a sleeping lion, emanating a scent of danger and slumbering power all the more potent because it was unconscious.

When he made a low sound deep in the back of his throat, Holly stepped back in alarm. Then she realised that he was simply dreaming. She fought down an unwelcome pang of concern and debated what to do. Should she wake him or just leave him to sleep? Heaven knew, he needed the rest, but he couldn't be very comfortable in that chair. And even now he had a wad of documents loosely clutched in his fingers. At least she could relieve him of those.

She tried to slip them gently out of his grip, but the movement brought him awake. He jerked upright and looked at her with bemused eyes. A gleam of recognition lit his face.

'We did it, honey!' he muttered thickly. 'They accepted our bid last night. I'm the new owner of Swanee Cotton. Aren't you going to congratulate me?'

Holly lost her temper.

'No, I'm not!' she snapped. 'You may be the new owner of Swanee Cotton, but you don't have a brain in your head when it comes to taking care of yourself. Don't you realise it's bad for your health to drive yourself like this? Now get out of that chair at once, go and wash and I'll fix you a proper breakfast. And don't give me any back-talk about it!'

A twitch of amusement quirked the corners of Simon's mouth.

'Hey, I thought I was the boss around here!' he protested,

'Then think again!' retorted Holly. 'And move it, buddy. I'm not kidding!'

When he returned ten minutes later, it was obvious that he had washed, combed his hair and even shaved. But he hadn't bothered to put on his jacket and tie, so that he had a more casual air than usual. If they were living together, he would probably look like this in the mornings, thought Holly, and sternly repressed an urge to slide her hands down inside his open shirt-front. With a disapproving sniff, she set a bowl of fresh fruit salad on the boardroom table and swept aside a pile of papers.

'Eat!' she commanded. 'And if you dare look at a paper while you're doing it, I'll run you through with the fruit knife.'

He gave a low growl of laughter. 'I wouldn't dare!'

'Good. Because when you finish that, I have a few more things to say to you about stress, nutrition and the way you're behaving.'

'Aren't you going to eat with me, Holly?'

'No.'

'Oh, come on. It's bad for my stress levels to have you standing there glaring and waving a knife at me.'

She had to smother a sudden impulse to burst out laughing. Simon was so obviously manipulating her with his pleading expression and soulful blue gaze.

'All right, then. But only on condition that you taste this food. I'm tired of seeing you look as if you're eating sand.'

Soon they were both embarked on a luscious concoction of watermelon, peaches, cantaloupe, honeydew and yoghurt. After that Holly fetched hot blueberry muffins and fresh coffee.

'Decaffeinated,' she said firmly.

'It's really very good,' Simon complimented her. 'Now do you want to hear about my takeover?'

Holly gave an exasperated sigh.

'Not particularly,' she said. 'I'm really not very interested in money. Besides, I think takeovers are horrible. Why do you want to gobble up some unfortunate smaller company when you already have so much of your own?'

Simon's mouth tightened.

'You're obviously talking about something you don't understand,' he growled.

Holly tossed her head defiantly. There might be a grain of truth in that. She had always thought of people who engineered takeovers as being rather like huge white pointer sharks, that cruised around with big, vicious teeth looking for smaller fish to engulf. But was it really like that?

'All right. So explain it to me,' she said.

Simon's face suddenly looked as absorbed as if he were engaged in stalking a wild deer or luring a trout from hiding. Holly had already set a Lazy Susan turntable in front of them so they could both reach the food without effort. Now, frowning thoughtfully, he picked up a silver teaspoon and set it on the turntable.

'Suppose this little spoon is the company I'm after,' he said. 'It's not a bad little company, it makes a good product, cotton fabric, and there are good people working for it, but it's badly undercapitalised. It doesn't have enough money to buy new equipment or to expand. Now, a big company like me comes along and takes it on board and away we go.' He spun the turntable. 'Suddenly the little company's products can go anywhere in the world. It opens a lot of opportunities for it. Instead of just making cotton fabric, the people there can make bedsheets, cotton furnishings, all kinds of things. It's no longer just a small-town bit-player; now it's got the chance to be a star on the international stage. Is that a bad thing?'

'No, I suppose not,' admitted Holly warily.

'And I'll tell you another thing,' added Simon half to himself. 'That company was about to go under if I hadn't taken it over. More than fifty people work for it, some of them family men and single mothers with kids to support.'

'So you really did it for them?' asked Holly hesitantly, feeling a rush of unexpected warmth towards him.

But the admiration in her voice only seemed to antagonise Simon. His lips twisted into a jeering smile.

'There's no need to look at me with that dewy-eyed expression of hero-worship, Holly,' he said in a hard voice. 'I'm not Mr Wonderful trying to solve all the world's problems, you know. And I don't want you getting the idea that I am. That takeover was a damned good move for me financially. I'll make a lot of money out of it.'

Holly felt wounded by the sarcasm in his voice. He had picked up a pencil and was rolling it between his fingers, watching her all the time with a contemptuous, patronising weariness as if she were a poor, stupid, little girl who still believed in fairy tales.

'I don't understand you!' she burst out. 'You seem to want me to have the worst possible opinion of you.

You're deliberately trying to convince me now that you're completely heartless. Aren't you? Aren't you?'

The pencil suddenly broke under Simon's fingers with a loud, snapping sound. He stared down at the pieces for a moment with a brooding expression and then dropped them on the table.

'Maybe,' he agreed lightly, as if he were bored by the intensity of her tone. 'Anyway, forget the takeover. Why are you so mad with me, Holly?'

She bit her lip, shrugged, struggled to deal with the conversation on his terms. For a moment she had felt as if they were poised on the brink of genuine communication, but now Simon was deliberately drawing her away. Back to the safety of meaningless banter and caressing compliments where the sexual attraction between them was nothing but a dangerous, enticing game. All the same, she felt the lure of it, as potent and fierce as the undertow of a hidden current in a gleaming blue sea. In her attempt to resist its spell, she found her words coming out as prim and disapproving as a nanny's.

'Because you're ruining your health the way you go on,' she replied. 'You need more rest, more relaxation.'

Simon gave a mirthless laugh and helped himself to more coffee.

'I play squash twice a week,' he announced.

'Squash?' said Holly contemptuously. 'Do you know how many men have heart attacks playing squash? If you ask me, that's just more of the same thing. More competition, more stress. What you need is to go away somewhere and unwind.'

Simon's face took on an abstracted look.

'You could be right,' he said slowly.

'Isn't there anywhere you could go away for a few days?' continued Holly. 'Somewhere really peaceful?'

The faraway look in Simon's blue eyes deepened.

'Yes, there is one place,' he agreed.

'Then go,' urged Holly. 'It would do you good.'

'Maybe I will,' he retorted with a sudden laugh. 'Any more orders, ma'am?'

Holly's eyes flashed. She knew he was taking the mickey out of her, but she wasn't going to be stopped from speaking her mind. She answered him in the tone of voice she would have used to Amber in one of her more fractious moods.

'Yes, I have. I think you should go home today and get some rest and don't come back here until you've had a good long sleep.'

'Well, if I promise to do that,' he said, gazing at her from under half closed eyelids, 'will you have dinner with me?'

Holly hesitated, feeling suddenly trapped. Her first impulse was to agree. Not because she thought Simon was trying to open up a serious relationship with her. Nothing like that. She could see perfectly well that he was amused by her motherly concern and quite happy to indulge her in any way she wanted. But even that mocking invitation was dangerously tempting. It would be fun to go out with him, to play this dangerous, glittering game of flirtation that he was offering her so enticingly. And surely she was old enough, wise enough, badly hurt enough not to fall for it? If she went into it with her eyes open, wouldn't it be safe enough just to have a few harmless dates with him? To enjoy his intoxicating, virile allure without losing her head and falling wildly in love with him? The pause grew longer and then she remembered Heather's words of warning.

'No, I can't,' she said in a rush. 'I don't think it would be right. I don't think we ought to get involved in any kind of personal relationship.'

Simon's keen, blue stare unnerved her.

'Yet you're ready enough to tell me how to run my life,' he mocked. 'Doesn't that imply a certain level of personal relationship?'

Holly caught her breath.

'I'm sorry,' she stammered. 'I know I shouldn't have said those things to you. I just don't have the right. I'm only an employee.'

Simon's gaze flicked her as lazily as if he were a fisherman casting a line into a particularly promising stream.

'Don't say that,' he drawled so blandly that Holly hated him. 'Whatever you are to me, Holly, it's not just a pair of oven gloves and a spitfire temper.'

The following day Simon arrived at her apartment at noon, looking every inch the impassive, controlled businessman again. Glancing at his untroubled blue eyes and his expressionless mouth, Holly could scarcely believe that he had ever done anything to cause her such turmoil. Even his smile was brief and rather abstracted.

'I have another job for you to work on, if you're interested,' he announced without preamble. 'Can we discuss it?'

'Sure. Come on in.' Holly swallowed her disappointment at his brisk manner. He didn't even seem to notice that she was wearing a blue dress that fell in soft folds, flattering her figure. 'What's it all about?'

'I've decided to take your advice and have a few days' holiday. Well, not exactly a holiday, because I can manage to combine it with some work I need to do. What are you laughing at?'

'Nothing,' choked Holly, pulling a straight face with an effort. 'Go on.'

Simon gave her a suspicious glance before he continued.

'I'm planning a four-day cruise upriver and into the bayoux, leaving on Sunday. I thought you might like to come and cook for me.'

'But where would we stay...? Who would be...?' Holly floundered hopelessly.

Her panic seemed to afford him a sardonic amusement.

'Oh, don't worry,' he said quizzically. 'You'll have plenty of chaperons, if that's what's concerning you. About half the people who were at the dinner at my house will be along with us. Including Joan Reynolds, my secretary.'

Holly was conscious of a feeling of mingled relief and disappointment.

'But what's it for?' she asked. 'You said there was some work you had to do?'

'That's right. I need to prepare a suitable album cover for a CD of Cajun music that I'm bringing out soon, so I'm taking a photographic crew into the bayoux with the musicians to try and find a suitable backdrop. Have you ever been into the bayoux, by the way?'

'No.'

'But you know what they are?'

'Bits of waterway that have wandered off from a big, slow river?' hazarded Holly.

'That's right. The bayou country around the Mississippi is famous. Full of alligators and swamp grass and cypress forests covered in Spanish moss. And the Cajun people who live there are great, really warm and hospitable with their own distinctive brand of music that dates back over two hundred years. They're descended from French settlers who were driven out of Canada by the British in the eighteenth century and they've kept their old culture intact. You'll love it out there.'

His face was suddenly animated and Holly felt the familiar excitement surge between them as his gaze met hers. It was as if he was trying to share something immensely important with her.

'It sounds fascinating,' she said honestly. 'How do we get there?'

'I have a paddle steamer which I normally lease out for tourist cruises. We'll take that upriver as far as Perier and use it as our base.'

'But you can't take a paddle steamer into the swamps, can you?' Holly demanded in bewilderment. 'Wouldn't it run aground?'

Simon's eyes narrowed in amusement.

'Of course it would,' he agreed. 'But the steamer won't be going into the bayoux, it will stay safely on the Mississippi. We'll hire a flat-bottomed boat for the swamp part of the trip. That way the photographers can take a good look around until they find a scene that suits them.'

Holly blinked.

'It seems like a lot of trouble just for a photo,' she exclaimed.

'Believe me,' Simon assured her, 'nothing is too much trouble for a CD that's going to sell millions of copies. Besides, when I'm working on something I like to get every detail perfect. Including the food for the expedition.'

Holly smiled wryly.

'If that's a compliment, thank you,' she said.

'It is. And you're welcome. Will you cook for us?'

She hesitated.

'Four days away from New Orleans,' she worried aloud. 'It all depends on whether Sophie can manage at the restaurant without me.'

'She can,' Simon assured. 'I already telephoned and asked her. And, of course, I'll make it worth your while.'

Holly frowned, annoyed at this high-handed management of her affairs. But there was no doubt that her sister needed the money and Betty Mae would be happy to take care of Amber. All the same, she wasn't going to let Simon win his victory too easily.

'I'd have to see the cooking facilities,' she quibbled.

'No problem. I'll take you there right away.'

The boat was moored on the riverside, and appeared to be a miniature version of one of the paddleboat steamers that were so popular with tourists. It was three decks high, painted white with a yellow gingerbread trim lining its top deck and the roof of the bridge, with a red paddle-wheel on its stern, and twin metal funnels surmounted by what looked like two ornate crowns. Once aboard, Simon took her on a brisk, conducted tour of the vessel, showing her everything from the wheelhouse gleaming with brass and mahogany, to the guest cabins on the upper deck, and the vast saloon on the lower one. It was here that Simon called a halt.

'I don't know about you,' he said. 'But I'm starving. Why don't we have some lunch, and then you can take a look at the galley, and tell me whether you want to accept my proposal?'

'All right,' agreed Holly warily. 'Thank you.'

She let Simon usher her into a comfortably upholstered dark red dining chair, and looked around her with interest. The saloon was nearly sixty feet long and took up the full width of the vessel. At the far end in the bow of the ship was a comfortable sitting area with deep couches, a dark blue carpet and polished coffeetables. In the centre of the room was a parquet dancefloor and a platform for a dance-band. Beyond this, in the area where Simon and Holly were now sitting was the dining section with one large table and three smaller ones. This part of the boat more than any other made Holly feel as if she had stepped into a time warp. The tables and chairs were of solid mahogany, the large portholes were framed by chintz curtains with a dark red floral pattern, and even the lights set into the woodpanelled walls at the end of the room were in the shape of sconces with artificial candles. The table in front of them was set for two with a starched damask table cloth, Spode china, gleaming silver cutlery, and a cut-glass bowl of red and white roses. As Holly continued to stare, a door in the wood-panel wall opened and a black man in a chef's outfit came gliding out to meet them.

'Hello, Jason,' said Simon pleasantly. 'This is Miss Thomson. She may be coming on the cruise with us next week to do the cooking. I'd like you to give us some lunch and then show her over the galley if you would.'

'My pleasure, sir. How do you do, ma'am? Can I get you both something to drink?'

'A gin and tonic for me, please,' said Holly.

'And a Scotch and soda for me.'

It was pleasant to sit back and enjoy the chill, bitter flavour of her drink, and the discreet luxury of her surroundings. The air-conditioning purred softly, sending waves of cool air into the room and the muted sound of blues music wafted from concealed speakers in the living area. In spite of her initial wariness, Holly felt her guard begin to slip, and she even gave Simon a quick, uncertain smile when he raised his glass to her.

'Well, here's to a pleasant cruise,' he said. 'Now if you've no objection, I'll get Jason to bring us whatever he has simmering on the stove in the galley there. He's an excellent cook, and he specialises in Cajun food. Does that suit you?'

Holly nodded.

'That would be fine,' she agreed.

It was fine. Jason brought them corn soup with tomatoes and river shrimp followed by Cajun fried chicken with rice and green salad, and a peach shortcake for dessert. While they ate, Simon questioned her about herself.

'You said you flew in from Hawaii,' he asked. 'Is that where you live normally?'

'Yes,' agreed Holly.

'So are you planning on staying long in New Orleans?'

'I'll stay as long as Heather needs me,' she replied simply.

Simon's eyebrows drew together.

'That's very touching,' he commented.

Holly stared at him suspiciously, but she could see no sign of irony. Her right hand, which had been clenching the silver soup spoon, slowly relaxed.

'Well, we're a close family,' she explained. 'Heather would do the same for me. Any of them would.'

'Any of them?' said Simon, raising his eyebrows. 'How many of you are there?'

'Five. My parents, my brother Mike, Heather and me.'

'And have you always lived in Hawaii?'

'Mainly,' she agreed. 'But my Dad was a chef in the US navy for years, and he really got bitten by the travel bug, so when he left the Navy we got dragged around all over the place until he decided where he really wanted to settle. I've spent a lot of time in Sydney, too. That's my mother's home town. She's Australian.'

'What made you become a chef?' asked Simon.

Holly's eyes danced.

'Greed, mainly. I'm very fond of eating, and both my parents are terrific cooks. Besides, it seemed like a good way to see the world. A chef can usually get a job anywhere.'

'So your father's not the only one with the travel bug, eh?' teased Simon.

'That's right. After I finished my training in Sydney, I worked in some big hotels in Australia and later in Honolulu. And I had a year travelling around in Europe. I've never had any trouble getting a job.'

'So it was no problem to you uprooting and coming to New Orleans?'

Holly shook her head.

'No.'

'Don't you have a boyfriend waiting for you back in Honolulu?' quizzed Simon.

She looked at him sharply, but he was busy buttering a piece of his bread roll, with a convincing air of indifference. No, she didn't think he was being nosy. Just making conversation. But the question brought a flood of unwelcome memories. She thought of Dennis, and her throat constricted.

'No!' she said with unnecessary sharpness.

Simon's blue eyes rose lazily to meet hers. She was suddenly aware of the tension in her body, of the way her lips were pressed together so tightly she was trembling, of an irrational desire to race out of the saloon and be done with men forever. Hating him for this sense of turmoil, she went on the attack herself.

'How about you?' she demanded. 'Have you always lived in New Orleans?'

'Yes. My mother's family has been here for over two hundred years.'

'Do you have any brothers or sisters?'

She wondered what had caused the change in Simon's face. His expression was suddenly stormy and turbulent. Was that because of conflicts with his family? Or shouldn't she even have asked?

'Look, I'm sorry,' began Holly. 'I didn't mean to——'

'It's all right,' cut in Simon, holding up his hand to silence her. 'I'm not sensitive on the subject. But I guess you could say I'm a loner. I certainly don't seem to be cut out for family ties.'

Holly felt an obscure sense of pain at this blunt statement, and she was horrified to hear her next words.

'Haven't you ever been married?'

Simon gave her a rather startled look, as if taken aback by this question. But then his eyes narrowed.

'No. I've never found anyone who made it seem worth while. Have you?'

Holly thought of Dennis again. And immediately found herself in that tangled thicket of emotions that had trapped her for the last year. Bewilderment. Pain. Anger. Relief?

'Once,' she said in a troubled voice. 'Well, almost. I thought we were going to be married but it didn't happen. And I'd need to be very certain ever to risk it again. Look, I'm sorry, how did we ever get on to this? It's my fault, isn't it? Why don't you tell me what you want me to cook next week?'

She felt nervous and flustered at the way Simon was eyeing her so unblinkingly from the other side of the table. But fortunately at that moment Jason arrived to take away their empty soup bowls and she was saved from any more difficult revelations. When the cook arrived with the fried chicken, she changed the subject deliberately.

'This is delicious,' she said. 'How does he get it so crisp?'

Simon smiled absently.

'Well, the traditional Cajun way is to float a match on top of the heating oil,' he said. 'When it lights, that means the grease is hot enough to start cooking.'

Holly shuddered.

'I don't think I'd be brave enough to try,' she exclaimed. 'I'd be afraid of sending the whole galley up in flames.'

After that, they chatted amiably about various meals they had eaten and about Cajun cooking. To Holly's relief, Simon didn't ask her any more questions about her private life, and she began to breathe more easily. In fact, when they finished the delicious peach shortcake with strong black coffee and Simon proposed a visit to the galley, she agreed with enthusiasm. Jason was busy loading the dishwasher and watching a soap opera on a TV set built into the overhead cupboards, but he paused in his work to show her around. Holly couldn't help being impressed by the efficiency of the compact space. There was a four-burner cooker, a multi-function electric oven, twin circular sinks, a fridge, freezer, dishwasher, and loads of cupboard space.

'It's wonderful!' she exclaimed approvingly.

'Yes, ma'am,' agreed Jason. 'You're going to enjoy working here, I know I always do.'

A thoughtful look came into Holly's eyes as she said goodbye to Jason, and followed Simon up on deck. After the pleasant coolness of the boat's interior, the outside air settled on her skin like a warm, moist blanket. And yet Heather's shabby apartment, broken air-conditioner and all, suddenly seemed like a welcome refuge. When Simon stopped near the gangplank and took both her hands in his, it was all she could do not to snatch herself out of his grip and run for safety. She swallowed hard, hoping he wouldn't notice how clammy her fingers felt or the tremor in her legs.

'What's wrong?' he asked, gazing at her intently.

'Why don't you just ask Jason to come on the cruise and cook for you?' she blurted out.

A faint, mocking smile flickered on his lips.

And for one shocked moment she wondered if the engines had leapt into life and the paddle-wheel had started churning. But it was only the racing of her own heart as Simon lifted her hands to his lips and kissed them.

Try as Holly might, she couldn't see any sign of turbulence in his face to match her own. 'Jason's going on vacation next week,' he said mildly. 'I asked you to take his place because——'

He paused.

'Because?' she prompted, her heart racing so hard she felt it must burst out of her chest.

'Because I knew you needed the money,' was the disappointing reply.

CHAPTER FIVE

I MUST be insane, thought Holly a few days later. Certifiably insane. All that man has to do is breathe on my knuckles, gaze soulfully into my eyes and I get myself into a mess like this! What is wrong with me? Am I losing my mind?

She gave the hashed brown potatoes in the frying-pan a vicious stir, turned down the heat and stared stormily out through the door of the galley into the dining-room. In different circumstances she might have thoroughly enjoyed this trip. After all, the paddlesteamer was quaint, charming and utterly luxurious, most of her fellow passengers appreciated her cooking and she was seeing the Mississippi River in the pleasantest way imaginable. But there was one fact Holly hadn't known when she'd agreed to come on this cruise. That Virginia Cox would also be aboard.

A strong smell of burning bacon recalled Holly to her duties. Hastily she turned down the gas under the second frying-pan and lifted the crisp, fragrant pink curls on to a plate before putting them in a warming tray. Cutting the potatoes into quarters, she turned them over to brown and fried four eggs in the bacon fat. Then she made up the trays, snatched off her apron and moodily tidied her hair. The last thing in the world that she felt like doing at this moment was taking breakfast in bed to either Virginia or Simon. But that's what you get for letting strange men kiss your hands! she told herself savagely. And it's all part of your job. You're just a glorified kitchenmaid, remember?

How could she forget after the fiasco of the previous day's events? Grimacing, she let her thoughts drift back...

The cruise had begun well enough and Simon had even been on deck to greet her as she came aboard. Although his face was guarded, the gleam of pleasure in his blue eyes was unmistakable as he took her arm and led her from the bright, humid warmth of the deck to the vessel's cool, shady interior.

'John,' he called, motioning to a steward in a white uniform. 'This is Miss Thomson. I'd like you to take her bag to the Number Three stateroom on the second deck. Holly, come and get a cool drink and meet the guys.'

'The guys' proved to be Simon's secretary Joan Reynolds, who gave Holly a friendly smile of recognition, two photographers, Tom and Carla, and four musicians, Martin, Sam, Robert and Scott. They all made Holly welcome and the steward brought her a glass of iced tea.

Gazing around at the circle of friendly faces and listening to the good-humoured banter that flew back and forth, she felt glad that she had come. Her eyes suddenly met Simon's and a little skip of excitement and apprehension disturbed the even rhythm of her heartbeat. Well, a bit confused and hesitant maybe, but still very, very glad. Deep down inside her she felt certain that she was going to love every minute of this trip.

Her certainty lasted exactly twenty-four minutes, until Virginia Cox came aboard. By this time the group in the saloon had become almost uproarious. Anecdotes were trotted out concerning various wildly unlikely disasters at concerts, there were shouts of laughter and spirited bits of improvisation on the piano and frequent requests for more beer and iced tea. Then suddenly there were the unmistakable sounds of an arrival on deck. Footsteps on the gangplank, three dull thuds as if heavy luggage were being set down and a high, rather schoolmistressy voice giving orders.

Simon, who had been in the middle of a story involving a taxi-chase half way across London in pursuit of a misguided saxophone, paused in mid-sentence.

'That will be Virginia,' he announced, rising to his feet. 'I'd better go and welcome her aboard. Don't expect me back for a while. I have a few sales figures from Frankfurt that I want to discuss with her.'

It was Martin the violinist who spoke for all of them when he walked over to the piano and played a few resonant, bass bars of a funeral dirge.

'Well, that's it, guys. Looks like the party's over.'

Over the next few hours Holly felt that Martin was right. From the moment Virginia arrived, the party really did seem to be over. It was not as if she was actively rude. In fact, she even complimented Holly on the brownies which she served for afternoon tea. But in some subtle way she managed to introduce a class distinction which hadn't existed aboard until her arrival. When Holly was laying the tables for dinner on that first evening, Virginia turned to Simon at the far end of the saloon and spoke in an audible stage whisper.

'Simon, don't you think we ought to invite Miss Thomson to join us for dinner tonight? After all, it's a fairly informal party, so she shouldn't be too much out of her depth. And it would be a kind gesture.'

Out of her depth, thought Holly, bristling with resentment. Kind gesture. Thank you so much, *madame*! Even Simon's terse reply didn't do much to soothe her ruffled feathers.

'Yes, of course, Virginia!' he said impatiently. 'I had no intention of doing anything else. Anyway, Holly's no fool. She knows where she belongs.'

Do I? wondered Holly bitterly, later that evening as she stood in the galley loading the dishwasher. And what did he mean by that anyway? That I'd never be fool enough to try and escape from the kitchen where I belong? Or that I'd never be fool enough to think that I did belong in the kitchen? Oh, I hate her! And I hate him, too. I wish I knew what was going on between them...

But this was maddeningly difficult to discover. At dinner that night Simon and Virginia behaved in a way that baffled Holly. They seemed to be a couple and yet their relationship was strangely low-key. Holly had scheduled dinner for eight o'clock and Simon and Virginia arrived together in the saloon at seven forty-five for pre-dinner drinks. The paddlesteamer's crew had already finished eating an hour earlier, but John, the chief steward, a lanky twenty-three-year-old with warm brown eyes and wiry hair, had remained on duty to help Holly. As she bustled about the kitchen putting the finishing touches to the shrimp cocktails, he glided into the saloon to wait on Simon and Virginia. Pausing in her work, Holly peeped through the partly open galley door and what she saw made her heart sink.

The four musicians and Joan Reynolds were all dressed in casual, comfortable clothes and Holly herself was wearing a bright blue Hawaiian-printed dress under her white apron. But Simon and Virginia looked more as if they were going out to a formal dinner party. Simon was wearing a lightweight grey suit, cream shirt and blue and grey striped tie while Virginia looked exactly as if she had stepped off the front cover of *Vogue*. Her blonde hair was drawn back into a chignon and she was clad in a severely cut black dress that showed off her pencil-slim figure and the expensive gold necklace which matched her earrings and bracelet. As Holly watched, they both accepted cocktails from John's tray and sat down together on a couch. Holly felt a ripple of amusement and relief as Simon suddenly produced a folded spreadsheet from the inner pocket of his jacket. But her relief turned to disquiet as he unfolded it and Virginia wriggled closer to him to look at the data. Something about the way she laid her hand on his shoulder and sat with her leg pressed against his was strangely disturbing. Not obviously flirtatious, no, not that. And yet it was the sort of matter-of-fact intimacy that a couple might show who had been married for so long they took each other for granted. With an effort Holly wrenched her thoughts away from them and back to the subject of her work. Snatching off the apron which somehow made her feel like Cinderella, she picked up a trayload of shrimp cocktails and went out into the dining area. Once the table was set she cleared her throat.

'Excuse me, everyone. Dinner is ready.'

They all wandered over and sat down at the table. John hovered silently in the background, pouring white wine as they began talking and eating. Virginia turned to Holly with a wide, glowing smile.

'This cocktail sauce is absolutely delicious, Miss Thomson,' she said. 'You must tell me how you make it.'

But just as Holly was opening her mouth to reply, Virginia turned back to Simon and began talking about pie charts and European markets. Seeing Holly's disconcerted look, Joan Reynolds took pity on her and leaned across the table towards her.

'Tell me, my dear,' she said in a friendly voice. 'Someone said that you came from Hawaii. Is that correct?'

'Yes, that's right,' agreed Holly.

'Well, I'm planning a vacation there next winter. I'd be really grateful if you could tell me the best sights to see.'

Holly had just embarked on a vivid description of hula dancing when Virginia suddenly interrupted her.

'Oh, do you come from Hawaii? Whereabouts?'

'Oahu,' said Holly briefly.

'Really?' purred Virginia. 'What a coincidence. My brother has a beach house on the waterfront just near Walmanalo Beach. It's a beautiful spot. Just imagine, Simon, twelve rooms, every one with a wonderful view over the ocean and you can hear the waves roaring all night long. You ought to come on vacation there with me some time, darling. Do you know the area, Miss Thomson?'

'Yes, I do,' agreed Holly curtly, reflecting that Virginia's brother must be a multimillionaire to afford a beach house there.

'And do you live anywhere near there?' continued Virginia, still in the same velvety, purring voice.

Holly took one look at the other woman's face, registering the cool, superior smile, the blue eyes narrowed in amusement, and felt hotly convinced that Virginia was doing this deliberately. How better could she show up the gulf between her social status and Holly's? Holly's frayed nerves snapped.

'No, I don't,' she said defiantly. 'My parents own a small apartment overlooking the Likelike highway. You can hear the traffic roaring there all night long. As for me, I used to rent an even smaller apartment overlooking a laundromat.'

The annoyance in her voice was unmistakable and Simon gave her a startled frown. Virginia flashed him a rueful 'Oh, dear, isn't she touchy?' look and then spoke again in an exaggeratedly soothing voice.

'I'm sorry. I didn't mean to offend you, Miss Thomson.'

'I'm not offended. And please call me Holly. Everyone else does.'

Trying hard to control her simmering annoyance, Holly rose to her feet and began clearing away the serving bowls with swift, jerky movements. She was conscious of everybody's eyes on her as she made her escape to the galley. John gave her a sympathetic, questioning look as she set down the tray full of used bowls.

'What's wrong?' he asked in a low voice.

'Oh, nothing,' replied Holly through her teeth. 'Maybe I'm being too touchy, but I keep feeling that Virginia is patronising me. She talks to me as if I'm some lower form of life.'

John's large hand came out and gripped her shoulder.

'Hey, take it easy,' he urged. 'Even the lower forms of life have it pretty good around this place. Simon's a nice guy to work for. We have terrific food, fine accommodation and——' he kicked the door shut '—a nice, private galley for big, schmaltzy hugs when life gets too much for us.'

Holly giggled protestingly and fought him off, but her good humour was restored. A moment later, straightening her hair and feeling as if she had just emerged from a tumble-drier, she opened the door and stepped into the dining-room with a tray full of main courses. To her surprise she found Simon watching her frowningly as she and John began to hand out the plates. Drawing in breath in a ragged gulp, she vowed to control herself a little better during the remainder of the meal.

She succeeded so well that she found herself almost totally left out of the rest of the conversation. Oh, Joan and the musicians complimented her on the food. Even Simon said that the swordfish steaks were delicious. But that didn't stop Holly from feeling more and more depressed as the evening wore on. As she listened to Virginia telling witty anecdotes about her student years at Radcliffe, her skiing holidays in Gstaad, her statistics professor in college and her family's summer home in Vermont, she no longer felt that it was merely a table that separated her from Simon. It was an abyss, growing wider by the minute, a social gulf that could never be bridged. And Simon belonged on the other side of it with That Woman, who was obviously his natural mate.

After all, it was Virginia who had the looks, the intellect, the wealth, the family background, the social grace to captivate a man like Simon. Not Holly. Even the Bombe Alaska, a triumph of blue flames, pointy meringue and deliciously chill ice-cream was not enough to console her. The moment everyone had finished their dessert and coffee, she sprang to her feet and began clearing away the plates.

'Why don't you get John to do that?' asked Simon.

'I can manage, thank you,' she replied curtly, dropping her eyes.

She no longer wanted to look at him. Heather was right. Whatever he was after, it sure wasn't marriage and Holly had no intention of being a rich man's plaything a second time round. Shooting Simon a glance of pure dislike, she hurried away to the kitchen. It was about time she did the only thing she was fit for and washed the dishes.

'Let me take those, Holly. You go back and take it easy for a while. I got everything under control here.'

John's slow, Southern drawl was infinitely comforting. And the discovery that the galley was already spotless and the dishwasher loaded made Holly feel like bursting into grateful tears. Instead she waited until John had set down her tray, then flung her arms around him and kissed him.

'You are such a nice guy, John!' she cried.

A footstep sounded behind her and she whirled around to see Simon watching her with a coldly disapproving expression.

'Oh, I'm sorry!' she said, recalled to her role as employee. 'Did you want something? More coffee maybe?'

'No, thank you,' he replied in a cold, clipped voice. 'I simply came to inform you that I want my breakfast on a tray in my stateroom at six a.m. sharp tomorrow. Virginia's requirements are the same.'

And with that he stalked out of the room, closing the door with a bang.

So now I've got to take him breakfast in his cabin, thought Holly resentfully next morning. And there'll be an atmosphere between us that you could cut with a knife. Damn him, damn him! Damn them both! Picking up the first of the trays, Holly marched into the dining-room where a couple of the crew members were eating an early breakfast. John leapt up from the table to help her.

'That was a real nice breakfast, Holly,' he said appreciatively. 'Now where can I carry this for you?'

Holly's face softened into a smile at the young man's kindness.

'It's for Miss Cox. Thank you, John. I'll bring the other tray for Mr Madigan.'

The steward escorted her to the pantry near the upstairs staterooms before bidding her a cheerful goodbye. Holly picked up the first of the trays and knocked on the door of the stateroom just to the right of the stairs.

'Come in.'

Virginia's voice sounded as brisk as if she were in an office. And she had obviously done her best to transform the attractive cabin into precisely that. Floral curtains closed off the large portholes so that there were no distracting glimpses of the river, every available surface was littered with books and papers and Virginia herself was propped up against a pile of pillows typing vigorously on a laptop computer. At Holly's entrance, she looked up, removed her tortoiseshell glasses and sighed.

'Oh, it's you, is it? Well, just put the tray on the bedside locker. Carefully... if you don't mind. I'm too busy to eat yet, but I'll get to it as soon as I can.'

Holly's blood boiled at the ostentatious way Virginia shrank from her as she set down the tray. Does she think I drop everything I carry? she wondered furiously. For a brief moment she toyed with the tantalising image of letting an avalanche of cantaloupe wedges, bacon, hash browns, fried eggs and coffee cascade all over Virginia's navy silk pyjamas, but some remnant of sanity restrained her. Regretfully she moved aside a couple of weighty volumes and put down the tray.

'You should eat the eggs while they're fresh, madam,' she remarked mildly.

'Thank you for the advice. Mind you don't bang the door as you go.'

Gritting her teeth, Holly stalked out of the room. But when she knocked at Simon's door two minutes later, she had the disconcerting sense that the same scene was repeating itself. Oh, the décor was different. Wooden shutters in place of the floral curtains, masculine navy and white striped cushions on the sofa, a severely tailored navy bedspread. Other than that, everything looked exactly the same. Like Virginia, Simon was propped up on a pile of pillows and typing on a laptop computer. The bedspread around him was littered with papers and he barely glanced up at her entrance. Instead he went on frowning ferociously at the data on his screen. Holly rolled her eyes and uttered a muffled groan.

'What are you snorting about?' demanded Simon, looking up.

She kicked the door shut behind her and strode across the room, trying to act like a stewardess and not succeeding.

'Nothing,' she replied in a tight, exasperated voice.

'Don't give me that garbage. You're mad as hell about something. Tell me what it is.'

Setting down the tray, Holly hunched one shoulder in a resentful shrug.

'Look, it's nothing. I'm only an employee here, I've no business having opinions.'

With a ruthless sweep of his arm, Simon thrust the computer across to the far side of the bed. Then he grabbed Holly's wrist and brought her whirling down on to the bed. Sheets of paper fluttered in a blizzard around them and Holly found herself flat on her back, gazing up at Simon with wildly dilated eyes. He crouched above her, holding her wrists and breathing fast and hard.

'Forget "employee"!' he growled. Then suddenly his mouth came down on hers in a kiss that electrified her.

Whimpering in protest, she struggled for a moment and then surrendered blissfully to the sensations that were sparking through her. Molten fire seemed to blaze through every nerve ending in her body and the warm pressure of Simon's body on hers awoke an aching need deep inside her. She felt her eyelids flutter shut and was dimly aware that she was sighing and swallowing as his lips quivered down over her pulsating throat. Arching her back, she felt her nipples tingle into hard, aroused peaks that strained against the thin cotton of Simon's pyjamas. He swore violently under his breath and one powerful masculine hand suddenly released her wrist and plunged inside her flimsy T-shirt. Ruthlessly evading the confining fabric of her bra, he cupped her warm, throbbing flesh in his fingers and began to caress it. She gasped at the excruciating thrill of his touch and made an irresolute movement as if to escape.

But the truth was that she really didn't want to escape. This might be madness, but if it was madness, she wanted more. More, more, more. Simon's face was only an inch or so away from hers. So close that she could hear his harsh, uneven breathing and see the way his eyes looked down at her, dark and strange and glittering. Through the weightless barrier of their clothes she could feel the violent thudding of his heart and the insistent stirring of his masculine arousal. When he raised one hand and caressed her cheek in a slow, sensual whorl, she turned her head and bit his thumb softly. He shuddered and uttered a low growl in the back of his throat.

Then with an abrupt movement he hauled himself off her and strode across the room. For a moment he stood with his back to her and his head bent. His shoulders heaved as he fought to regain his composure.

'W-what's wrong?' she faltered.

He swung round violently, his face suffused with anger. His dark blue eyes flashed alarmingly and a muscle was twitching in his cheek.

'Hell's teeth!' he exclaimed. 'Do you flirt with any man who lays a hand on you?'

Holly choked at the unfairness of this. Simon's abrupt transition from passion to moral outrage shocked her as deeply as if the ground had suddenly opened under her feet. Part of her wanted to protest that no man had ever aroused her with such intensity. But rage held her back. Damn him! She wouldn't give him the satisfaction of letting him know that. Besides, he had no business saying such a thing to her, however tempestuously she reacted to his caresses. What did he know of her dealings with other men? Nothing! So why should he insult her like this?

'What are you talking about?' she flared.

'I'm talking about you and John Beattie, the ship's steward! You only met the guy yesterday and you're probably already sleeping with him!'

Holly fought down a wild impulse to burst out laughing. Simon was still glaring at her and yet even that anger was deeply arousing. To her shame she felt an unwilling pulse of excitement throb through her as he took a step closer.

'Aren't you?' he seethed.

'No, as a matter of fact, I'm not,' she replied with all the dignity she could muster.

'Then what are you doing with him?' he demanded.

'That's none of your business,' she said quietly. 'But I'm not sleeping with him. And I've no intention of discussing it any further.'

Something in her tone seemed to convince him, for after a moment's indecision, he looked her straight in the eye. Raising one finger, he jabbed fiercely at the air.

'Look,' he began. 'I had no intention of... All I wanted to... Hell, what's the use?'

With an exasperated snarl he marched across to the two seater sofa and slammed his hand into a pile of folders, sending them crashing to the floor. Then he slumped into the cleared seat and buried his face in his hands. For an instant Holly could see nothing but his glossy dark hair and his tensely knotted fingers, then he raised his head and looked at her. As an exercise in self-control, it was remarkable. Most of the anger and frustration had vanished from his face, leaving only a wary shrewdness in his blue eyes. Most, but not all. In spite of his attempt to look calm and friendly, a telltale stiffness about his jawline and a narrowing of his eyes made it clear that Simon's annoyance—or passion?— still smouldered below the surface. Yet his voice was deliberately conciliatory.

'Tell me what you were thinking when you came into the cabin,' he ordered. 'Before you started that nonsense about being an employee.'

But Holly still hadn't forgiven him for his outburst.

'Do I have to?' she enquired sweetly. 'Is it part of my job description?'

Simon swore under his breath and his black eyebrows drew together in a scowl.

'You know damned well that your being my employee has nothing to do with what's going on between us,' he exploded.

'Hasn't it?' she challenged.

'No.'

'So what am I supposed to do when I bring breakfast to your cabin and you start mauling me?'

'*Mauling* you?'

This time his oath was so loud and so outrageous that Holly's eyes widened in shock. Springing to his feet, Simon stalked across to the bed and seized her by the wrist.

'Are you telling me that you responded to me the way you did because you're my employee?' he rasped. 'That you think your little performance was part of what I hired you for? That I do this to any woman who works for me?'

His rage was so intense that it almost scorched her. For a moment she tried to fight back, to meet those pitiless blue eyes glare for glare. But some spark of honesty made her drop her gaze.

'No,' she muttered.

'I'm glad to hear it,' he said savagely. 'Because let me tell you, sweetheart, whatever is happening between us is happening out of honest attraction, not for money.'

Holly's senses reeled. The words 'sweetheart' and 'honest attraction' rang in her head like tolling church bells. She blushed, swallowed, stared up at Simon in agonised uncertainty.

'What are you trying to say?' she demanded hoarsely.

He drew one finger down her cheek and smiled bitterly at her.

'That if your kisses are only motivated by fear of losing your job, I wish you'd tell me right now. You can take your money for the cruise and a generous sum in compensation and catch the next boat back to New Orleans with my apologies for insulting you. Is that what you want to do?'

Holly opened her mouth and then closed it. Too late she saw that Simon had trapped her. If she said 'yes', she would be on her way immediately with a golden handshake, and one glance at Simon's tight-lipped mouth told her that he would never try to contact her again. But if she said 'no', it was as good as admitting that she wanted the relationship between them to continue. To develop. Was that really what she wanted?

'Well?' he barked. 'Do you want to leave?'

Holly dropped her gaze.

'No,' she muttered.

His merciless finger lifted her chin.

'Look at me,' he ordered in a hard voice. 'And let's get one thing straight. We're both here because we want to be. And I don't employ women just so that I can seduce them. Right?'

'All right!' flared Holly. 'But let's get something else straight while we're at it. I don't leap into bed with any man who lays a hand on me and you've no right to suggest that I do! For heaven's sake, who do you think you are to insult me like that? You don't know a damned thing about me!'

He took in breath in a deep, shuddering gulp. His fingers locked in her hair and he squatted down in front of her so that he was looking straight into her eyes.

'No, you're right, I don't,' he admitted hoarsely. 'But I intend to find out. Starting now. Have you eaten breakfast?'

Holly gave a muffled groan of laughter.

'No, I haven't. But what's that got to do with anything?'

'Not much, except that I've just realised that I'm starving and this food you've cooked is getting cold. Will you stay and share it with me?'

Holly shifted uncomfortably.

'I should get back to the galley. The others——'

'John can look after them.'

She smiled, twisted a curl around her finger, ducked her head shyly.

'All right.'

Without taking his eyes off her, he rose to his feet, took the silver covers off the tray and began dividing up the breakfast. Holly winced to see her carefully arranged food being so ruthlessly shovelled about. Yet when Simon handed her a laden plate and his fingers brushed hers, she felt a tremor of pleasure at the contact.

'Eat,' he urged. 'And then we'll talk.'

The cantaloupe was sweet and cool and refreshing. And even the eggs and bacon and hash-brown potatoes, although now rather lukewarm, were tasty and filling. Simon produced a spare glass from the bathroom for the orange juice, but when they reached the coffee, there was a problem.

'There's only one cup,' said Holly. 'Do you want me to go get another one?'

Simon's lips puckered thoughtfully.

'We could share,' he suggested.

The intimacy of it was vaguely shocking. As if we really knew each other well, thought Holly. As if we were...lovers.

'OK,' she agreed breathlessly.

They discovered that they both liked coffee the same way. Sweet and black and strong. After they had shared two cups, Simon frowned at Holly.

'All right,' he said with mock severity. 'Now tell me what the hell you were snorting about when you first came bursting in here.'

Holly sighed.

'Just that you don't seem to have changed at all. You came away for a rest and you're still working as hard as ever. I also thought that you and Virginia made a good pair. I took her breakfast in before yours and she seemed exactly like your twin. Sitting in bed typing furiously and looking all cold and efficient and hard as nails, far too busy with serious things to enjoy anything as vulgar as food!'

Simon's face grew suddenly bleak.

'Is that how you see me?' he challenged. 'Cold and efficient and hard as nails?'

Holly blushed, suddenly aware that she had been very tactless.

'A bit,' she admitted. 'Well, not exactly. I mean, underneath you seem as if you're really smouldering with impulses, but it's all kept totally under control. Oh, I can't explain!'

'On the contrary. You explain extremely well,' said Simon grimly. Turning his back, he strode across the room. 'And you're right about Virginia too. In many ways we do make a good pair.'

Holly stared at him in consternation.

'You're not——'

'Lovers?' He swung round. 'Why? Would it bother you if we were?'

'Of course it would!' she retorted hotly. 'I happen to believe in honesty and commitment in relationships. Do you think I'd want to do what we just did with somebody else's man?'

He folded his arms and frowned at her, his head tilted on one side.

'No. I suppose not,' he admitted at last.

Their eyes met and held. Simon seemed to have no compunction about scrutinising her and Holly had the uncomfortable feeling that he was gazing right into her soul. Suddenly she realised that he still hadn't answered her question. Her throat constricted, but she had to know.

'Are you and Virginia lovers?' she asked hoarsely.

His gaze skewed away from hers. Abruptly he shifted his position and strode around the cabin, clenching and unclenching his fists.

'I'm not prepared to discuss that,' he growled. 'All I'm prepared to say about Virginia is this. There is nothing in my relationship with her to prevent you from spending time with me.'

Holly felt a torment of uncertainty grip her stomach. She wanted to believe Simon and yet she had the uneasy suspicion that he wasn't telling her the truth. Or at any rate not the whole truth. But before she could tackle him about it, he suddenly changed the subject.

'Oh, forget Virginia!' he exclaimed impatiently. 'Look, why don't you come out into the bayoux with us today instead of staying on the boat and cooking? I think you'd enjoy it and there are lots of interesting things I could show you. What do you say?'

Holly hesitated. If I had any sense, I'd tell him to push off and I'd go and shut myself in the galley, she thought despairingly. I know I'm playing with fire, but somehow I just can't wait to get burnt. She ran her tongue along the curve of her lower lip.

'Yes,' she said.

CHAPTER SIX

IT WAS steamy in the bayoux. Hot and green and lush, shrill with insects, teeming with wildlife, rank with warm, rotting vegetation. And Holly loved every minute of it. As the flat-bottomed boat skimmed slowly over the glassy green water, she hung over the railing and eagerly watched the scenery glide by. Whatever destruction was being wrought elsewhere, this part of the swampland was a world almost untouched by man. Most of the time the only signs of human presence were the throbbing of the outboard motor and the occasional glimpse of an old-fashioned Cajun cabin perched on piles a few feet from the water's edge. Dense stands of cypress, tupelo and pines grew right to the water's edge and, along the banks, thickets of brown reeds offered shelter to numerous birds. Where the water was at its shallowest sunlight penetrated easily and skeins of green algae floated on the surface. Once Holly's heart almost stopped as she saw an alligator glide into a sluggish stream with no more than a faint, secretive splash. And several times she saw graceful egrets soar into flight on lacy, white wings at the boat's approach.

All the tension of the last couple of weeks slowly began to ebb away and she found herself feeling peaceful and optimistic. It was true that nothing had really been resolved between her and Simon. She was still no closer to fathoming the relationship between him and Virginia. Nor could she be sure that he wanted anything more than a brief, tempestuous affair with herself. Yet the decision to live dangerously had infused her with a dizzy sense of exhilaration and sharpened enjoyment.

Not everyone shared her mood. The boat's tin roof might provide some shade, but it seemed to magnify the merciless heat of the sun's rays. And the open sides of the vessel were an irresistible invitation to large, juicy mosquitoes. The two photographers were stoical about the discomfort of their assignment and the four musicians only voiced humorous objections, but Virginia kept up a non-stop barrage of complaints.

'How much longer until we get there, Simon?' she demanded at last in an exasperated voice.

Simon, who was standing in the stern with one hand on the tiller of the outboard motor, shrugged complacently.

'No more than half an hour, Virginia. Don't worry. Paul will have a nice cool drink ready and waiting for us.'

'Well, I hope he does,' grumbled Virginia. 'If I'd known this boat wasn't air-conditioned, I would never have come.'

'Pity you didn't know,' muttered the accordion player under his breath. Then he spoke aloud. 'Is that where we're going, Simon? To Paul Raveill's place?'

'Yes. His cabin is about the most authentic Cajun scene I can think of. It should make a great photo for the album cover.'

Holly saw what he meant about twenty minutes later when he cut the boat's motor and let it drift up alongside a weathered grey wooden jetty projecting out into the water. No more than a stone's throw away stood a primitive cabin built out of the same weathered timbers as the jetty. It had a shingled roof, a shady veranda, a brick fireplace on one outside wall and dark wooden shutters at the windows. But in spite of its shabbiness, the home was obviously cherished. A neat picket fence marked off a tiny front garden full of palmetto trees, blue ageratums, bright red and yellow nemesias and white balsam. And a whimsically carved wooden alligator lurking on the bank near the front gate showed that the owner had a sense of humour. As Simon was tying up the boat, a man of about sixty with a grey beard and twinkling brown eyes appeared on the front veranda.

'Welcome, welcome,' he called in a booming voice. 'Come out in back and have a cold drink before you all melt.'

They scrambled ashore and Holly found her hand firmly grasped by Simon as he led her into the front garden.

'You haven't met Paul properly, have you, Holly? This is Paul Raveill. Holly Thomson.'

Holly smiled warmly at her host.

'Oh, I know you!' she exclaimed. 'You were at Simon's dinner party at Chartres House, weren't you?'

'That's right,' he agreed, taking her hand from Simon's grip and clasping it. 'And you were the little lady in search of the Curaçao, weren't you? Well, you put it to very good use, honey. That was one of the best meals I've eaten in a long time.'

'Thank you,' murmured Holly.

She felt rather taken aback by the way Paul's quizzical glance moved from her to Simon and back again, almost as if he could guess what had passed between them that morning. Simon stood rather stiffly, deliberately aloof and looking away from Holly. The older man gave a throaty growl of laughter and pinched her cheek.

'Well, well,' he said genially. 'I hope I'll be seeing a lot more of you.'

She was saved from answering by a shout from Tom, one of the photographers.

'Hey, Simon. There's some great props in the back yard. Come and take a look at this and tell us what you think. It should make a terrific photo.'

They all trooped around to the rear of the house to view Tom's discoveries. Sure enough, the spacious backyard held a treasure trove of homely Cajun artifacts. A weathered grey chicken-roost on stilts with a ladder leading up to it, an old-fashioned sugar-house with a brick oven beneath a shingled roof, a wagon that had seen better days, old wooden barrels held together with rusty hoops, a grindstone sitting on the porch of a timber outbuilding.

'Isn't it great?' enthused Tom. 'Why don't we get the guys to put on their Cajun clothes, grab their instruments and take some shots up there on the porch? That'll blow people's minds!'

Yet somehow neither of the two photographers was satisfied with the result. Holly sat in the relative coolness beneath a spreading magnolia tree and watched as the four musicians, two photographers and Simon marched about, waving their arms, moving equipment and arguing.

'Can't they hurry up?' complained Virginia. 'This heat is unbearable!'

'Have another glass of orange juice,' urged Paul, gesturing at the generously laden table which he had set out under the tree. 'Or something to eat.'

Virginia's gaze flicked over the orange juice, potato chips, French bread, cold shrimp, watermelon and stuffed tomatoes set out in a mismatched assortment of old crockery on a blue and white checked cloth.

'No, thanks,' she replied listlessly.

Holly saw the sudden shadow in the elderly man's eyes and wondered uncomfortably whether his feelings were hurt. Poor old thing! He couldn't help being poor and she hated to see his hospitality rejected so ungraciously.

'I'd like some more juice, please,' she said, smiling warmly at him.

He gave her a conspiratorial wink and poured a tall glass of the sweet, chilled liquid for her. But at that moment Virginia found another cause for complaint. A high pitched whining sound was followed by a yelp and a loud slap as she mashed a mosquito on her arm. Leaping to her feet, she glared at Paul.

'I don't know how you can stand this!' she exclaimed. 'Can I go inside?'

'Of course, my dear. But there's no air-conditioning.'

'No...?' Virginia looked appalled and then shrugged irritably. 'Well, anything's better than this, and of course your cottage is wonderfully quaint. I'll take my tape recorder and note down my impressions of Acadian life. It doesn't look as though much has changed since the eighteenth century.'

Tom, the photographer, lounged up to the table and made a face at Virginia's departing back. Picking up a hunk of crusty French bread, he bit into it and shook his head.

'There's something about that woman I just don't like,' he exclaimed in a muffled tone. 'I can't believe Simon is really planning to marry her.'

Holly felt suddenly cold. Her knife dropped against a tin plate with a loud clatter.

'Oh. I—is he?' she asked in a wobbly voice.

'That's nothing but gossip,' said Paul sternly, pointing his own knife at Tom. 'And you shouldn't be repeating it. I know it was what Simon's mother wanted, but that doesn't mean he'll do it. He's a grown man, perfectly capable of making up his own mind about who he wants to marry. Now stop talking foolishness and tell me why you haven't taken a decent photo yet.'

Tom ran his hands through his bushy red hair and sighed.

'I dunno. Everything we do seems kind of flat. Lifeless. I'm not sure why.'

Holly was too preoccupied with her own miserable, churning emotions to pay much attention to what the two men were saying. But she was dimly conscious of Paul's shrewd brown eyes boring into her and she tried to smile at him. Suddenly he slammed his palm down on the table, setting the plates rattling.

'Lifeless, eh? All right I know what we want—a good Cajun party to get us moving. And it will brighten you up too, my dear. Come with me and we'll get it organised.'

To Holly's amazement she found her hand engulfed in Paul's massive grip and, with a shouted explanation to Simon, he dragged her off to his battered swamp boat.

'We'll go to my neighbours across the bayou first. Matt Clement and his mother. Young Matt loves music, he'll soon put the word around.'

Young Matt proved to be a wiry, dark fourteen-year-old, who was speechless with delight at the invitation. Within half an hour they were back at Paul's place accompanied by twenty people, most bringing food and musical instruments. Soon the lively rhythms of fiddle, piano accordion, washboard and harmonica rang out above the whistles and chirps of the local wildlife and a riotous party was in full swing. Tom and the other photographer crouched, snapping their cameras happily as exuberant dancers whirled past them. But Holly had no heart for the toe-tapping, hand-clapping, whooping activity that was trampling the green grass into muddy oblivion. She stood on the sidelines under the magnolia tree, swallowing hard and trying to ignore the ache in her throat. Simon seemed to be enjoying himself, she thought resentfully. He was out there in the thick of the dancing, looking more relaxed and happy than she had ever seen him. No doubt he was thinking about his future bride, Virginia!

'You're fond of Simon, aren't you?'

Paul's deep voice took her completely by surprise, and she jumped as he laid his hand on her shoulder.

'I thought I was,' she admitted miserably. 'But if he's going to marry Virginia...' She left the sentence unfinished.

'I hope he won't,' said Paul soberly. 'She would destroy him, that woman. Oh, on the surface Simon seems rather like her, much as I hate to admit it. Ambitious, hard-headed, even cold. But I know him better than most people and underneath he has passion and fire in his heart. The right woman would bring that out. A woman like you.'

'Me?' squeaked Holly in disbelief.

Paul's brown eyes twinkled.

'Yes, you, little one. You cook with a passion; is it possible you also love with a passion? Ah, you hesitate. Maybe you fear the pain of falling in love. But, believe me, it's worth the risk.'

'Is it?' asked Holly huskily.

'*Certainement*. And if it's Simon who is bringing that colour to your cheeks and making your eyelashes flutter so charmingly, I beg you, take the risk, *chérie*. Find out what you feel for him. Now why don't you go and dance together?'

Her thoughts in a whirl, Holly allowed herself to be led into the centre of the throng of people. Paul bundled her into Simon's arms as if she were a Christmas present and then threaded his way through the crowd to speak to Martin. Suddenly the music stopped and Holly found herself staring up at Simon. His eyes lit up as they met hers and his rather stern features relaxed into a smile that made her feel breathless. Lowering his head, he spoke into her ear.

'Are you enjoying yourself?'

'Yes,' she murmured and suddenly it was true.

The sound of Simon's hoarse baritone so close to her, the grip of his warm fingers holding her arms, the nearness of his muscular, virile body all combined to make her feel slightly intoxicated. She had the giddy sensation that the ground was moving under her feet, then realised it was only because Simon was spinning her round to face the musicians. Paul was standing in their midst, holding up his hands for silence.

'Mesdames, messieurs. I have an announcement to make. I want to play you a new piece I've just finished composing. It's a love rhapsody. And I want everybody to get up and dance to it in pairs.'

The notes of the violin wailed through the air in a slow, melancholy tempo that was unbearably poignant. Holly's eyes filled with tears as Simon drew her close against him and they began to dance. Somehow she had never imagined that he would be a good dancer. He had always seemed too restrained, too tense, too reluctant to let himself go. Yet now she found herself swept along with a force and passion that enthralled her. Simon didn't merely dance to the music. He was the music, at first haunting and sad and unbearably melancholy. And then, as Paul made an abrupt change of mood and rhythm, Simon too was transformed. Now the notes spilled violently forth at amazing speed, full of fire and dash and extraordinary staccato jerks and pauses. She found herself cast at arm's length, wrenched back, flung into the air and spun wildly in an exhilarating frenzy of rhythm and speed. Faster and faster Paul played until Holly was gasping for breath. And still Simon led her deeper and deeper into this astonishing world of motion and energy until the music reached an abrupt climax and he caught her against him. She stood, sweating and shuddering, aware of the powerful thudding of his heart through his damp shirt, of the way his hands were clutched convulsively in her hair. It seemed like an eternity that they remained unmoving and then a ripple went through the crowd and they all turned to Paul, cheering and clapping.

'That's great, Paul!' shouted Simon. 'I'll book you in for your next studio session right away.'

'Let me get a drink first,' begged Paul.

Yet as they moved towards the table under the magnolia tree, Holly discovered that not everyone was delighted with the performance. It was true that Martin gave her a sly wink as Simon guided her through the crowd, but there was another watcher who was not so well pleased. Virginia Cox had come out of the cabin and was standing utterly motionless on the back porch staring directly at her with an expression of frozen rage on her face. Too late Holly realised that Simon still had his arm firmly around her shoulders. Not wanting to provoke a scene, she wriggled out of his grip. But Virginia's hackles were already up. Marching down to the table, she gave Simon a cold smile.

'Shouldn't we be getting back now?' she suggested. 'After all, poor Holly will need time to prepare dinner, won't she?'

Holly flushed at this blatant reminder of her inferior status and she felt the muscles of Simon's arm tense involuntarily. Yet, even if his eyes were stormy, his voice remained cool and polite as he answered Virginia.

'Yes, you're right. We should. Have you boys got enough photos now?'

'Sure,' agreed Tom. 'Too bad my best shots are all of Paul, though. I guess we can't put a photo of him on Martin's album cover.'

'I don't mind if you do,' said Paul, with a sly chuckle. 'But Martin might.'

'You betcha I would,' agreed the violinist. 'I'll tell you what though, Paul. I'd really like to have the music of that violin piece of yours so I can learn it. Do you have a copy?'

Paul groaned.

'C'mon, buddy!' he retorted. 'I'm just a simple fisherman. I can't read music. It only exists in my head. If you want to learn it, you come out here and I'll teach you.'

The trip back to the paddlesteamer was uneventful. Simon was in the stern steering the boat, so at least Holly was spared the ordeal of having his arm around her while Virginia glared at them. But that didn't stop Virginia from casting her an occasional baleful glance. It was after four o'clock in the afternoon when they finally returned to the paddlesteamer and it was obvious that there was a storm brewing. Charcoal-grey clouds massed overhead and the air was hot and damp and oppressive. With the menacing skies and the disturbing looks she was getting from Virginia, Holly was only too glad to vanish into the coolness of the galley. As she began frying chicken and making potato salad, she heard the confused murmur of voices in the saloon next door. Everyone seemed to be busy. Simon and the two photographers were discussing the day's shooting with his secretary, the four musicians were tuning up for a jam session, and Virginia was still dictating notes about her impressions of Acadian life into a small tape recorder, but gradually the uproar subsided. Virginia announced that she was going up to her cabin to look for some books, Simon and the two photographers withdrew to the living area at the far end of the saloon and, after a lot of shuffling, moving of music stands and equipment, and playing of very sour notes, the four musicians launched into a lively Cajun tune. Humming under her breath, Holly went out into the dining area with a platter of fried chicken and stopped dead. To her annoyance Virginia had left papers, books and pens all over the main dining table.

Setting down the fried chicken, Holly hastily tidied the table and bundled all the offending objects onto a couch at the far end of the room. Then she came back, finished setting the table and put out the rest of the meal. She was just gazing down in satisfaction at the spread of fried chicken, potato salad, green salad, asparagus and hollandaise sauce, corn on the cob and watermelon wedges when Virginia suddenly appeared beside her.

'Excuse me, Holly,' she said. 'Have you seen my tape recorder?'

Her tone was sweet, but with an accusing undercurrent that grated on Holly's nerves.

'No, I'm sorry, I haven't. But I just bundled up all your books and papers and put them on the couch in the saloon. I suppose it could be in with those.'

'It's not. I've already looked.'

This time the irritation in Virginia's voice was unmistakable.

'Well, I don't know where it is!' retorted Holly curtly. 'The only other place I've been is the galley and I didn't see it there. But you're welcome to look if you like.'

'Maybe I will,' agreed Virginia, and marched into the galley while Holly and the musicians exchanged eloquent glances.

Nobody really expected Virginia to find anything, so they were all taken by surprise when there was a sudden cry of triumph from the galley.

'Got you! What on earth do you think you're doing, you thieving little wretch?'

Everyone crowded to the door of the galley and looked in. In the middle of the room a dark-haired boy of about fourteen dressed in bleached, cut-off jeans and a faded cotton shirt stood guiltily clutching a piece of fried chicken and eyeing Virginia apprehensively.

'You're the boy who was at Paul's party this afternoon, aren't you?' exclaimed Holly. 'Matt Clement—isn't that your name?'

'Matt Clement?' echoed Simon's deep voice. 'What the hell are you doing here, kid?'

The musicians melted away at Simon's approach so that only four people were left in the galley. Matt, Virginia, Holly and Simon. The boy wriggled uncomfortably in Virginia's grasp and hung his head.

'I'm sorry,' he said in a hoarse adolescent voice. 'I didn't mean no harm. I had to come to the store for my dad and then I heard the guys playing some music so I sneaked on board to listen. I'm real sorry.'

'I'll bet,' snorted Virginia. 'Sneaked on board to see what you could steal, more likely.' Her gaze alighted suddenly on a tattered denim bag dropped on one of the counter tops. A small, knobbly shape was visible through the thin material. 'What's in that? Is it by any chance my tape recorder?'

'No!' cried the boy hotly. 'I ain't no thief.'

'You were thieving that fried chicken. I caught you at it.'

'Oh, don't be silly, Virginia!' cried Holly. 'A teenage boy snitching a wing of fried chicken isn't exactly grand larceny. The poor kid was probably hungry.'

'Well I want to know what he's got in that bag!' exclaimed Virginia. 'Let him show us if he's so innocent.'

Simon's voice intervened. Deep, measured with a hint of amusement.

'Do you mind showing us, Matt?'

Looking half defiant and half sheepish, Matt dropped the piece of fried chicken on a plate, wiped his greasy hands on his cut-off jeans and reached for the bag. Then, with the air of a magician pulling a rabbit out of a hat, he slowly brandished a harmonica. Simon gave a smothered hoot of laughter.

'Well, I think you're going to have to look elsewhere for your criminal, Virginia. Tell me son, can you play that?'

'A bit,' agreed Matt with a shy grin.

'Then come out to the saloon and give us a tune,' ordered Simon. 'I'd ask you to stay for supper, but I think you ought to be going before the storm breaks. Holly will make you up a parcel of chicken to take with you. Won't you Holly?'

Holly nodded, feeling touched by Simon's matter-of-fact kindness to the boy. She was just coming out of the galley with a brown paper bag full of chicken in her hand when Matt began to play, and she was totally unprepared for what was to follow. With a nervous starting glance at the assembled audience, the boy cupped his hands over his instrument, flicked his long hair back from his face, and launched into a superb rendition of the melody which they had all heard only that afternoon. Paul's rhapsody. Transposed from violin to harmonica. As the last notes died away there was a stunned silence, then Simon spoke.

'Where did you learn to play like that?' he demanded. 'Have you had lessons?'

Matt gave an embarrassed shrug. 'No, I just listen to people.'

'Well, you're good. Damn good. Are you interested in being a musician?'

The boy's eyes shone.

'Hell, yeah!'

'In that case I'm going to talk to your parents and arrange for you to have lessons. If you work your butt off for the next two years, I might have a recording contract for you at the end of that time. What do you say?'

'All *right*!' cried Matt joyfully.

'Do your parents have a phone?' asked Simon.

Matt shook his head. 'No. Costs too much.'

'Hmm. I guess I'll just have to come back with you. How did you get here anyway?'

'In a pirogue,' explained Matt.

'Well, what are we waiting for?' demanded Simon. 'Let's get going.'

Holly came forward with the bag of fried chicken and Simon looked at her as if he had suddenly remembered she was there.

'Do you want to come with us?'

Holly hesitated. She was still miserably conscious of Virginia's barely contained hostility and the atmosphere of tension that flared whenever the three of them were together. Wouldn't it only aggravate the problem if she went off alone with Simon? And yet what claim did Virginia have on her tact or good will or even her sense of common decency? It wasn't as if the history professor were Simon's wife or acknowledged girlfriend. Besides, she had never been more than barely civil to Holly. And this excursion might be a chance to find out more about the man who frankly intrigued her. Slowly, she nodded.

'Yes, please.'

Matt's pirogue turned out to be a light, narrow boat similar to a canoe with a couple of paddles stowed under the seat. As he scrambled aboard and fished these out, Matt looked at Simon doubtfully.

'Do you know how to paddle one of these?' he asked.

'Sure,' agreed Simon. And with the air of a man who is perfectly at home he picked up one of the paddles and scrambled into the stern. 'Sit in the middle, Holly,' he instructed.

As they skimmed through the still waters of the bayoux, Holly glanced over her shoulder at Simon from time to time. She was puzzled and intrigued by the new aspect of him that was now being revealed to her. As effortlessly as the teenager in the bow of the boat, he hauled and twisted on the paddle with a fluid, graceful motion that sent the boat speeding over the water. Once the boy looked over his shoulder and grinned. 'Hey, you're good at this,' he exclaimed. 'You seem like you've done it for years.'

'I have,' agreed Simon.

Holly's brain teemed with questions. When, why, how? She had always assumed that Simon was the product of a privileged background. The heir of a long line of plantation owners. And somehow, paddling through the swamps in a battered canoe didn't much fit in with that image. Was there more to him than she had suspected? More than the successful businessman that he seemed to be? Suddenly close by the boat, a plaintive wail, just like the cry of a human baby caught her attention. She turned her head and gasped as a dark, hairy shape suddenly dived beneath the water's surface.

'Ugh! What was it? A rat?' she demanded.

Simon gave a low growl of laughter and shook his head. 'No, a nutria,' he explained. 'You often hear them moving around at dusk and dawn, and they sound exactly like babies. They're a kind of fur-bearing rodent. Watch as he comes up and you might see his orange teeth.'

She obeyed, and was rewarded a moment later by a damp, furry face, with four vivid orange teeth like a beaver's. But how did Simon know so much about the inhabitants of the swamps? As they plunged deeper and deeper into the warm, steamy maze of waterways, she fired questions at him and was soon convinced that he was deeply knowledgeable about the bayoux and all its wildlife. It was almost a disappointment when the Clements' house came into view. It was nothing but an old 'shotgun', a barge dwelling with all the rooms in a single row, moored against the bank. And when they went inside to meet Matt's parents, Holly had another surprise. Although the conversation began in English, from time to time Simon slipped into Cajun French to emphasise a point or to make a more detailed explanation. The fisherman and his wife nodded doubtfully as Simon urged the importance of fostering the boy's extraordinary musical talent. But in the end, Simon's eloquence won the day and they agreed to let him pay for their son to have music lessons. The agreement was sealed with a glass of cheap red wine and then Simon announced that he and Holly must leave.

'How you gonna get back?' asked Matt's father in a worried voice. 'You know we're in for one hell of a storm.'

Simon smiled. 'I know. But if young Matt will just take us across the bayou to Paul's house, we'll ask Paul to drive us back to the river in his pick-up truck.'

But when they came ashore at Paul's jetty, they met with an unexpected problem. Matt was just paddling away towards his own house when the first fat rain drops came hurtling down like bullets, dimpling the grey surface of the water. Overhead there was a sudden roar of thunder like an aircraft taking off.

'Come on,' urged Simon, snatching Holly's hand, 'run for it or we're going to get soaked.'

As they went racing up the bank, the bombardment began. An avalanche of rain drops as hard and stinging as dried peas battered their unprotected heads and shoulders, and before they had even reached the gate in the picket fence they were both soaked through. The weathered cabin loomed up at them through a blur of falling water and as she scrambled, gasping and shuddering under the shelter of the front porch, Holly could already hear the roar of rain in the down-pipes. Turning back she saw that the bayou had been almost obliterated by the storm, and that the Clements' shotgun barge on the other side was no longer visible.

'Oh, I hope Paul's home!' she exclaimed, wringing the water out of her wet hair.

'Of course he'll be home!' insisted Simon confidently. 'Paul hardly ever goes anywhere.'

But as soon as they began hammering on the door of the tiny cabin, it became apparent that he was wrong. This was the one occasion when Paul had changed his habits.

'God damn!' exclaimed Simon in exasperation. 'What the hell are we going to do now?'

Holly gave a gasp of laughter.

'Swim?' she suggested.

'Maybe he's out in back in the shed,' suggested Simon.

But a hasty sprint into the uproar of the storm revealed that not only Paul was missing, but the pick-up had gone too. Simon returned drenched and swearing under his breath. 'He must have gone to Baton Rouge,' he said morosely. 'Well, there's only one thing to do.'

'What's that?' asked Holly, puzzled.

'Break in,' retorted Simon.

'Break in?'

Simon's white teeth flashed in a taunting smile.

'Sure. Paul wouldn't mind a bit of breaking and entering in a good cause.'

Holly wasn't so certain about that, but she didn't particularly want to stay on the porch for hours on end, so she made no objection when Simon went around testing all the windows and doors on the ground floor.

'All locked,' he exclaimed in disgust. 'Paul's got mighty suspicious in his old age. Well, there's only one thing for it, I'll have to climb up to one of the attic bedrooms.'

'Are you crazy?' demanded Holly, gesturing at the thunderous downpour that was still falling from the sky. 'There's no way you can get up there safely.'

'Sure there is. It's dead easy,' insisted Simon. 'Up the magnolia tree and along that skinny branch. I could do it blindfolded.'

But it was Holly who was blindfolded. After the first moment when Simon swung himself effortlessly up the trunk of the tree, with his eyes screwed half shut against the battering of the rain, she could no longer bear to watch. She was quite convinced that he was going to fall to a hideous death on the ground twenty feet below. And the sound of muffled cursing and scrabbling feet did nothing to reassure her. In the end she blocked her ears too, so it came as a great surprise when the front door of the cabin was suddenly flung open, and Simon appeared in the hallway, drenched and grinning. Never mind that he was secretive, baffling and downright infuriating. At least he was alive!

'Well, have you finished praying for me?' he demanded.

Holly let out a shuddering sigh, fell into his arms and hugged him tightly.

'You're crazy,' she moaned. 'Totally crazy. Anyway, what do we do now?'

His body was warm and damp and hard against hers, and his next words filled her with misgiving.

'Do? There's only one thing we can do. We'll have to stay the night.'

CHAPTER SEVEN

HOLLY felt her heart give a violent lurch at these words, and she darted a quick, panic-stricken glance at Simon, but he didn't look like a man who was plotting some elaborate seduction. For a moment he stood with his hands on his hips watching the storm with every appearance of enjoyment. His dark hair was plastered close to his head, his face was streaming and his wet clothes clung to his muscular body. And yet he seemed completely oblivious of Holly's presence. Narrowing his eyes, he gazed out with a fierce look of exultation at the drama of the storm. It was certainly worth watching. The sun had vanished completely and the murky gloom of the sky was lit up from time to time by vivid traceries of lightning. Beneath the crash and rumble of the thunder Holly heard the quieter sound of rain dripping from the eaves. Already the soaking torrents were bringing a new freshness to the garden, and the scent of flowers and damp earth came wafting on the air. Simon inhaled appreciatively and nodded as if he had been drinking a good wine.

'Well, let's open these doors and let some of the heat out,' he suggested practically. 'Then we'll get dried off and find something to eat.'

He flung open both the front and back doors, letting a current of rain-scented air filter through the house. Then he took Holly's arm.

'Let's go see what Paul has in his larder,' he suggested.

Holly hesitated.

'Won't he mind?' she asked doubtfully.

'Hell, no,' replied Simon with a hoarse chuckle. 'No Cajun would ever deny hospitality to somebody caught in a storm.'

All the same, Holly couldn't help feeling uncomfortable about the way Simon marched into the tiny house and made himself entirely at home. It was so dark in the kitchen that they could barely see each other's faces, and Simon groped for a box of matches and lit a kerosene lamp which was sitting in the centre of the table. The soft yellow glow filled the room revealing a scene that might have come from two hundred years earlier. In the centre of one wall was an old-fashioned black stove with a chimney leading up to the ceiling and a wooden food safe crammed into the alcove next to it. Opposite was a pine dresser crowded with old blue and white china, and in the centre of the room stood four battered, carved chairs and a small table covered in a blue and white checked cloth in a *fleur-de-lis* pattern. Other than that there was only a small sink with a single cold water tap, a few old cooking pots hanging from a decorative wrought-iron rack and two or three faded maps hanging from the walls. The walls themselves were made of handsawn pine planks, bulging and irregular in shape, but with a certain rustic charm. And the lamplight lent the room a cosy glow.

'Doesn't Paul even have electricity?' marvelled Holly.

Simon frowned.

'Yes, he does. In fact, he's a rich man from all his recording contracts. It's simply that he prefers lamplight and so do I. But I can turn on the overhead lights if you need them.'

Holly shifted uncomfortably, disturbed by his curtness.

'N-no, no,' she stammered. 'I don't need them. I just wondered.'

'Come upstairs and I'll find you a towel and something to wear,' urged Simon. 'You'll be relieved to know that there is a proper bathroom.'

The stairs were nearly as steep as a ladder and the bare wood in the centre of the treads was worn almost paper-thin by the passage of many feet. Once they reached the upstairs storey, Simon flung open a door on the left, revealing a room dominated by a huge, handcarved bed, covered with a burgundy and navy patchwork quilt. Apart from the bed, the only other furniture in the room was a plain mahogany chest of drawers topped by an old-fashioned wash-bowl and jug. In one corner of the room a few well-worn clothes hung from a rail half concealed by a shabby curtain. Other than that there were only bare, varnished floorboards and a small window set slightly crooked in the gable. It was stiflingly hot, and Simon strode across the room and flung open the window, letting in a rush of moist, fragrant air. Then he moved to the chest of drawers, opened one of them and began rummaging through the clothes.

'This is Paul's room,' he explained. 'I'll just see if he's got an old shirt or something you can wear.'

Holly gazed at him in dismay.

'We can't just take his clothes like that!' she protested.

But Simon paid her no attention. He simply went ahead until he found a faded cotton shirt which he bundled into her arms.

'Don't worry, I've known Paul a long time,' he assured her. 'Maybe I'll tell you about it one of these days.'

Touching her lightly on the shoulder, he propelled her into the tiny bathroom next door and handed her a large, almost threadbare towel.

'Why don't you get dried off?' he suggested. 'Come downstairs when you're ready and I'll fix you something to eat.'

Thoughtfully, she closed the door behind him and began towelling her hair briskly. Through the closed door she heard Simon's muffled footsteps as he went into the second bedroom, presumably in search of something to wear. In spite of his reassurances, Holly could not help feeling deeply perturbed about the way he had taken over Paul's house as casually as if he owned it. Did he always seize whatever he wanted without a second thought for other people? And if what he wanted was not a thing but a woman, would he simply take her with the same ruthless confidence? A shiver that was half alarm and half excitement ran down Holly's spine at the thought. Stop this, she ordered herself fiercely. You're just daydreaming! Being here alone with Simon doesn't really mean anything. It's just a minor glitch in his plans. He's being practical and sensible about it and so should you!

All the same, she could not help thinking about the way Simon had kissed her only that morning and, when she came downstairs and caught sight of him in the kitchen, she forgot all about being practical and sensible. Instead, she caught her breath in instinctive admiration. Unlike her, Simon wasn't dressed in one of Paul's old voluminous shirts. In fact, he was dressed in very little at all. He had found a faded pair of old, cut-off jeans rather like Matt Clement's and he was wearing them with the same negligent grace as the teenage boy. Except that Simon was no boy. His wide shoulders and powerful back rippled with muscle. In the lamplight he looked like some magnificent savage who had strayed in from the wild. Even his face was subtly altered. The usual preoccupied, guarded look had vanished and he seemed totally relaxed. Yet all the same Holly had the vivid sense of a dangerous, blatant sensuality, simmering beneath Simon's indolent exterior. At the sound of her footsteps he turned around and smiled.

'Hungry?' he demanded.

She saw that he was stirring something in a big iron pot at the back of the stove. A pot which was filling the kitchen with enticing, savoury aromas. Suddenly she realised she was ravenous.

'Yes, I am,' she agreed. 'You know, I cooked all that fried chicken and didn't get a single bite of it myself.'

Simon gave a low growl of laughter.

'Well, young Matt certainly made up for your lack of appetite. Now if you'd like to get some plates and cutlery, we'll eat in just a moment. And if you'll look in that innocent-looking food-safe down in the corner, you'll find there's a refrigerator hidden away there. Paul probably has the makings of a salad on hand. See what you can find.'

Holly investigated and found tomatoes and some lightly cooked asparagus. While Simon was busy at the stove, she quickly made up a tomato and asparagus salad with a vinaigrette dressing. A feeling of nostalgia swept through her at the sense of companionship in working side by side. And yet the pleasure was accompanied by a poignant twinge of sadness. After all, this wouldn't last. In a few hours, tomorrow morning at the most, she and Simon would go back to their separate lives. Simon to his business empire and Holly to... to what? Trying to save a dilapidated old restaurant from closure? Struggling to care for a five-year-old child whom she loved, but who wasn't even hers? Suddenly a pang of misery so piercing that it was almost a physical pain sliced through her. She caught her breath.

'What are you thinking?' demanded Simon sharply.

She made a face and busied herself with setting the table, her hands moving mechanically as she laid out a platter of crusty French bread, butter, the tomato and asparagus salad and waited for Simon to dish up the crawfish and rice. But he kept looking at her as if he were waiting for an answer to his question. In the end that silent scrutiny was too much for her.

'I was thinking that it's nice doing homely things like this... with somebody else,' she replied, stumbling over the words. 'It can be awfully depressing eating meals on your own.'

'Do you get lonely a lot?' he asked.

'Yes,' she admitted. 'Do you?'

His blue eyes met hers in a way that made her feel as if he were stripping her naked. It wasn't sensual, no not that, but hungry, penetrating, deeply disturbing.

'Not often. A man who works fifteen hours a day doesn't have a lot of time to get lonely. And I've never lacked for female company. To tell you the truth, I'm generally glad to find myself alone again.'

His smugness infuriated her.

'Perhaps that's because you've never bothered putting enough time and effort into a relationship to get the rewards from it,' she flared.

The disapproval in her voice was unmistakable and Simon's head jerked up as if she had slapped him. Suddenly he thrust the cooking pot away with a violent gesture and took three paces towards her. His hand, still unnaturally warm from the heated iron, touched her face, moved lingeringly down her cheek and caressed her chin. Her breath locked in her throat.

'Or perhaps it's because I've never found the right woman,' he muttered under his breath.

The room seemed to swim around her. She was acutely conscious of the warmth of his touch, of the way her heart was hammering and her legs were quivering so violently they would scarcely hold her. What was he saying? Surely he couldn't mean...? It was madness, pure madness even to think it. And yet his eyes were trapping hers with a fierce, demanding message that sent waves of faintness coursing through her. A message deeper and more primal than any words seemed to be pulsing between them, humming in the air, throbbing through her bloodstream. With a shudder of disbelief and deep, yearning excitement she suddenly felt that she recognised it. For one crazy moment she believed she knew what Simon was demanding from her. Not just sex, but a wild, explosive union of two souls and two hearts. A deep, primitive coupling of man and woman in a mating that would last a lifetime. Love in its purest form.

'Simon...' she breathed.

Her body swayed, her lips parted and she felt herself melting into his embrace. Then the image of Virginia flashed before her, bringing with it a storm troop of unwelcome emotions. Anger, suspicion, the refusal ever to be tricked and cheated by a man who might be after nothing more than a bit of enjoyable variety. Her whole body stiffened violently. Her eyes flew open.

'I-I think that crawfish is burning,' she stammered, recoiling from his touch. 'Perhaps we should eat before it gets spoiled.'

Simon's eyes narrowed and his lips twisted into a stormy line. For a long moment he gazed at her, then he turned his back on her as if she were no longer worthy of his attention. Lounging across to the stove with the indefinable menace of a prowling panther in his movement, he spoke curtly over his shoulder.

'Well, something certainly got spoiled, but it wasn't the crawfish. All right, Holly, let's play it your way. Let's make a lot of meaningless, polite conversation. That's what you want isn't it?'

She retreated into one of the carved wooden chairs and watched apprehensively as he set out the meal. There was a controlled violence in his movements as he set down the iron pot of crawfish on a wooden cutting board and opened a bottle of chilled white wine. Then with swift, furious neatness he sliced up the French bread and took his place opposite her.

'Go on, then!' he ordered brusquely. 'Talk!'

Her mouth opened slowly and then closed. She felt like a goldfish circling aimlessly in an aquarium. A flare of resentment went through her at the absurdity of the situation, but Simon was still staring at her with those implacable blue eyes and that taunting half-smile. His lean brown fingers drummed on the table as he waited for her to break the silence. She cast around wildly for something to say.

'It was awfully nice of you to be so kind to Matt.'

'Oh, I don't think you need to admire me too breathlessly about that. He's a very talented musician and I'll probably make a lot of money out of him one of these days.'

Holly felt an irrational sense of disappointment at this answer. Something about the way Simon sat looking so smug and debonair enraged her beyond measure. She couldn't believe that he was really as cynical and mercenary as he pretended and yet he seemed determined to prove that it was true. Didn't he care about anything except money and success?

'Is that all you ever think about?' she flared.

Simon's eyebrows rose sardonically.

'Apart from wanting you?' he challenged.

A wild colour filled Holly's cheeks.

'Stop it!' she croaked. 'Please. I can't handle it. Let's talk about Matthew. Anything. Was that really the only reason you helped him? Because you might make money out of him one day?'

Simon dug his fork into the smothered crawfish and tomato sauce then chewed and swallowed meditatively before he replied. His eyes took on a sombre, faraway expression as if he were gazing back through a long distance.

'No... not only that,' he admitted. 'He reminds me of myself when I was about that age.'

'But how can he?' demanded Holly in a startled voice. 'I can't see how you could possibly have had anything in common with him. You grew up in a plantation house in a wealthy family whereas Matt is growing up in the swamps in a family that's so poor it can barely support itself. What could you possibly have in common with him?'

'More than you might imagine,' retorted Simon curtly. 'I had a rough time in my teenage years.'

Holly snorted sceptically.

'Oh, yes? Had difficulty spending all your pocket money, did you? Or fighting off all the girls who were pursuing you?'

Even as she spoke, she was horrified to hear herself sounding so spiteful. But some demon of hurt pride and terror for her own survival was goading her on. All she knew was that Simon Madigan posed a mysterious threat to her own well-being, to her control over her feelings, her actions, the whole pattern of her life. Like a frightened animal she wanted to lash out, fight her way free, put distance between herself and her tormentor. Yet at least her attack demolished some of Simon's hateful self-possession. Uttering a low growl, he caught her by the wrist.

'Damn you!' he exclaimed. 'You're talking about things you don't understand.'

'Oh, I understand,' sneered Holly, snatching her hand away. 'I know that you grew up believing that the world owed you a living, that all you had to do was want something and you'd get it. It must be nice having such a cushy existence.'

'And do you think it's also nice to discover when you're fifteen years old that you're a bastard, that your very existence has caused trouble and heartbreak to the people around you?'

Holly stared at him in shock.

'W-what?' she faltered. 'What do you mean?'

Simon seemed suddenly preoccupied by the items on the table in front of him. He picked up a piece of French bread, crumbled it absently between his fingers and then set it down. Seizing his glass, he took a gulp of white wine and then grimaced, as if it were sour.

'I've never told this to another living soul,' he burst out. 'And I don't want it to go any further. But James Madigan, my mother's husband, wasn't my real father.'

Holly blinked.

'What? How do you know?'

Simon winced, as if he were already regretting his reckless announcement. But, having begun, he evidently decided to continue. Staring through Holly as if she weren't even there, he spoke in a low, abstracted voice.

'My mother was a very beautiful woman,' he said. 'Unfortunately she was also extremely hard to get along with. She was suspicious and critical of anyone who wanted to marry her, and always convinced that they were only after her money. The result was that she was a spinster until she was thirty-five. Then she fell in love with a penniless young musician, had a whirlwind love-affair, and became pregnant as a result.'

'Poor woman!' said Holly instinctively. The memory of her sister's unhappiness at a similar time flashed before her eyes and she winced. 'It's no joke being pregnant and unmarried. What did she do?'

Simon's face took on a stormy expression.

'In my opinion she made the biggest mistake of her life. My real father loved her and wanted to marry her, but she thought he was beneath her. She let her family talk her into giving him up, and marrying somebody else instead. The candidate they came up with was James Madigan. A wealthy widower with a pedigree going back three hundred years, a big legal practice and a dry-as-dust personality.'

'And you were the child?' prompted Holly.

Simon nodded.

'She never had another one. I think that embittered her. That and knowing that she'd given up the one man she really loved, all out of her own stupid pride.'

'So how did you find out all this?' demanded Holly. 'Did she tell you?'

Simon gave a mirthless laugh.

'No, she never told me a damn thing. I learnt it from James, my so-called father, on his deathbed. I was fifteen years old and he was dying of cancer and he thought I had a right to know the truth.'

Holly was silent for a moment, readjusting what she knew about Simon. A strange jumble of feelings overwhelmed her. Guilt, pity and a renewed rush of gratitude for her own infuriating but lovable family. Poor Simon! How much he must have missed. And did anyone ever get over that loss of security, that hateful sense of being unwanted? No wonder he had developed that cold, ruthless façade as a way of keeping other people at a safe distance! However much money and power and success he had, Simon Madigan was obviously badly scarred by his past.

'Did you ever meet your real father?' she asked curiously.

'Yes. I ran away and joined him as soon as I found out the truth. I lived in the bayoux with him for three years until I went to college.'

'In the bayoux?'

No wonder Simon could paddle a pirogue and speak Cajun French, no wonder he identified with a ragged teenager like Matt! But why? How?

'What were you doing there?'

'My father was a Cajun Frenchman, originally from Avoyelles Parish. Poor in everything except musical talent and human warmth. We had a cabin not two miles away from here.'

'Is he still alive?'

'Yes.'

'Do you see him now?'

'Yes. But he won't let me tell anyone that he's my father. He says he promised my mother that he would keep it secret and it's a matter of honour to keep his promise. According to him, it's also a matter of love.

Even now that she's dead, he still wants to protect her reputation.'

Holly's throat tightened.

'He sounds like a really fine man,' she said softly.

'He is,' agreed Simon. 'Although he doesn't altogether approve of me.'

'Why not?' demanded Holly with a touch of indignation. 'You've done well, haven't you?'

Simon smiled bitterly.

'Not according to him. His views are remarkably similar to yours. He thinks I waste too much time pursuing money and power and don't spend enough effort on the things that matter.'

Holly looked at Simon's grimly set mouth and thought of their past encounters, the constant sense of pressure and impatience that always seemed to simmer around him. Meetings, computers, takeover bids, deadlines. No doubt he was successful by most people's standards, but had it really brought him any happiness?

'Well, I think your father's right,' she said defiantly. 'You do waste too much time on things that don't matter.'

'But what are the things that really matter? Can you tell me that?'

The antagonism in his tone was unmistakable, but Holly flung up her head defiantly and met him, stare for stare. She sensed instinctively that his sarcasm sprang from some deep-rooted dissatisfaction with life. Yet she wasn't going to be bullied into sharing his cynicism. However naïve and ridiculous he might think her, there were certain things that she believed in and would always uphold. She thought of her family, always quarrelling but always loyal, of two or three close friends, of that achingly painful but deeply felt love affair with Dennis. Of her need for a love based on trust.

'Yes, I can,' she said quietly. 'At least I can tell you what matters to me. People. Love. Loyalty. Integrity.'

For a moment there was a spark of response in his blue eyes and he leaned towards her as if he agreed with what she was saying. A flare of warmth went through her and it was all she could do not to rush out of her chair and go to him. Taking in a small, unsteady breath, she smiled tentatively at him. Then the spell was broken.

'How touching,' he sneered, leaning back from the table and eyeing her mockingly. 'So, if we all learned to love each other, life would be perfect, would it?'

Scalding tears of frustration and rage sprang to her eyes. A moment before, she had felt such a wistful, tender yearning that she had almost believed she loved Simon. Now her feelings were different and much simpler. She wanted to kill him.

'Perhaps it would!' she agreed stormily, her eyes glinting.

'You're nothing but a romantic fool,' he said in exasperation.

'Thank you.'

There was a cold silence while they glared at each other.

'Have you ever been in love?' he demanded abruptly.

The question caught her unawares and for a moment she froze. A rush of painful memories came hurtling back to her. Those first carefree days on the beach with Dennis, parties, luaus, the seductive warmth of the tropics. Blue seas, the scent of a frangipani bush outside the window of his house the first time they had made love. The joy she felt when she thought she had found the man of her dreams. And the bitter pain of betrayal when Dennis had finally abandoned her. She shuddered.

'Yes,' she croaked.

'And did it live up to your expectations?'

His question was harsh, challenging, pitiless. And he clearly expected an answer.

'No!'

'What happened?'

She swallowed hard, fighting down the lump in her throat, gazing blindly round the room, trying not to let herself be overwhelmed by the familiar anguish.

'What's it to you?' she snapped.

'Let's just say I'm curious. Tell me, Holly. What happened?'

She paused, blinked, gave a shaky laugh.

'Oh, nothing important. I met Dennis several years ago. He'd come out to Hawaii to work for a big restaurant chain. We met on Waikiki Beach.'

'And?'

Holly shrugged.

'He invited me on a date. We went to a luau together... you know, a kind of Hawaiian barbecue?'

'Yes, I know. Go on.'

'After that we saw each other a lot.'

'Did you sleep with him?'

The question exploded into the room, as sharp and hard as a whipcrack. Holly caught her breath, suddenly conscious of the roar of the storm outside and of several quite irrelevant details. Like the lamplight gilding the dark hairs on Simon's arms and the way her heart was pounding so unevenly. And the strange thrill that went through her as Simon turned that stern, brooding look on her.

'Well, did you?'

She flinched, half hypnotised by the glitter in his blue eyes. Resentment filled her at this inquisition and yet she seemed powerless to resist it.

'Yes... I did.'

'How long did it last?'

'A little over two years,' she replied with a grimace.

'And why did it end?'

This was the point that always hurt her most. Not only because of her feelings for Dennis, but because she hated the thought that he had made such a fool of her.

'Oh, he was posted back to New York,' she said with a brittle attempt at indifference.

'And didn't you care? Didn't you try to follow?'

'Of course I cared!' she cried passionately, abandoning all pretence. 'I loved him, don't you understand, or I thought I did. And I believed he was going to ask me to marry him and go with him. Instead he...he...'

She bit her lip, unable to continue.

'He what?'

Seizing the jug, Holly poured out a glass of water with shaking fingers. Then she took a hasty gulp and blinked rapidly several times.

'Instead...he...told me 'Thanks for the good times, sweetheart. I'll never forget you, even when I'm back in New York and married.'

'*Married*?'

Holly nodded miserably.

'That's right. He'd had a girlfriend waiting in New York the whole time he was in Hawaii. Someone from the right kind of family. Rich. Pretty. And dumb. Just as dumb as I was! Totally unsuspecting. And he was going back to marry her.'

'That bastard!' exclaimed Simon hotly, slamming his hand down on the table. 'I'd like to strangle him with my bare hands.'

Holly swallowed another gulp of water and struggled to control herself. Tossing her head, she straightened her shoulders, drew in a long breath and met Simon's eyes.

'Would you?' she said sceptically.

He rose to his feet and paced around the room.

'Hell, yes! I think that was a really lowdown trick that he played on you.'

'Any more lowdown than the tricks you've played on women at various times?' she asked in a hostile voice.

'What's that supposed to mean?' he snapped.

'Well, you've had affairs with women and then broken up with them, haven't you?'

He stared at her, frowned and then glanced hastily away.

'Come on, Holly,' he replied uneasily. 'I'm thirty-four years old. What do you expect? Anyway, I never deceived them. I never pretended I had any intentions of marrying them.'

'Generous of you,' jeered Holly.

'Look, what is this about?' demanded Simon angrily.

'It's about what we were just discussing!' retorted Holly. 'Love. Loyalty. Integrity. How much of them do you offer in relationships?'

Simon made a strangled noise in the back of his throat.

'Not enough to suit you, obviously,' he said with heavy sarcasm. 'But then I suspect your standards are unrealistically high.'

'And I suspect yours are unrealistically low!' she whipped back.

He gritted his teeth and looked at her with blazing blue eyes.

'Thanks for the character reference,' he snarled. 'But what does it matter to you how low my standards are, Holly? After all, what you're trying to tell me is that you don't want a relationship with me in any circumstances. Aren't you?'

Holly flinched at the antagonism in his voice. And yet her brain told her that this was the moment she had been waiting for. The moment when she could order Simon clearly and distinctly to get out of her life. He would go, she knew that. And wasn't that what she wanted? After all, he was arrogant, domineering, ruthless, interested only in money and success. Yet, as he stood there gripping the back of his chair and looking at her with a gaze that scorched her, her heart went out to him. She didn't trust him as far as she could throw him, but there was something about him that moved her unbearably.

'Well?' he rasped.

She drew in a long, shuddering breath.

'I didn't say that,' she replied hoarsely.

He was round the table in an instant, cupping her face in his hands and gazing at her with hungry desperation.

'Holly,' he murmured.

With a rapid movement she jerked up her arms, breaking his hold.

'Don't try to sweet-talk me, Simon,' she warned. 'Before we go any further, I need to know exactly what you want from me.'

CHAPTER EIGHT

SIMON looked disconcerted.

'You know what I want from you!' he protested.

'Do I?' demanded Holly stormily. 'I'm not so sure about that. Why don't you spell it out for me?'

He shifted uncomfortably and his features creased into a resentful scowl.

'Well, I... You... Damn it, Holly, it's not easy to put into words!'

'Then let me give you some help,' offered Holly. 'Are you in love with me, Simon, or is it merely sexual attraction?'

Simon gave a harsh growl of laughter.

'Merely!' he exclaimed. 'There's nothing mere about the sexual attraction I feel for you, Holly.'

Holly couldn't repress a faint shiver of arousal at the searing glance he gave her but she kept her unruly responses strictly under control.

'You're going too fast for me,' she pointed out. 'And you still haven't told me what you want from me.'

'I want you!' retorted Simon, running his hand through his hair with a savage gesture. 'I want to hold you in my arms and cover you with kisses and make love to you until you beg for mercy. And in the morning I want to wake and find you beside me, warm and breathing and soft under my touch with that incredible hair of yours all bright and tangled across the pillow. That's what I want.'

Holly gritted her teeth.

'That's all very well!' she burst out. 'But what are your feelings towards me, Simon?'

'Feelings?' he echoed in an appalled voice.

'Yes.'

'I've just told you.'

'No, you haven't! Basically you've told me that you want to go to bed with me, that's all. If I gave you the slightest bit of encouragement, you'd be upstairs making violent love to me right this minute, wouldn't you? Wouldn't you?'

'Well, I... Yes! Damn it! Yes! And what the hell is wrong with that?'

Simon's hand slammed down on the table so hard that it made the plates rattle.

'Plenty!' howled Holly, leaping to her feet and storming to the far side of the room. 'You haven't even said a word about your feelings for me! Or don't you have any?'

'Feelings? Feelings!' raged Simon. 'Of course, I have feelings for you. I think... you're attractive... good company... sharp-tongued... feisty. I like you, Holly!'

A bitter smile twisted the corners of Holly's mouth at this strange recital of her virtues.

'That's not enough, Simon,' she said quietly.

'Why not?' he thundered.

'Because I've been hurt and abandoned once and I'm not fool enough to want it to happen a second time. The only way I'd ever go to bed with another man was if there was genuine love and commitment between us and I knew we were soon getting married.'

Simon's features twisted into a sneer.

'So it's love and marriage or nothing, is it?' he demanded sarcastically.

'God, I hate you!' hissed Holly. 'Every time you mention love and marriage, you spit them out as if they're dirty words.'

'Well, what do you expect?' snarled Simon. 'With the kind of background I had, there wasn't much to convince me that love was lasting or that marriage was anything very special.'

'Then I pity you,' whispered Holly. Suddenly a lump rose in her throat, so hard and painful that she could hardly breathe. 'Oh, what's the use? We're both wasting our time here—it's like talking a foreign language to each other. I'm going upstairs.'

'Wait!' In a swift movement Simon crossed the room and barred her way as she reached the door. 'We haven't settled anything yet.'

'Yes, we have,' said Holly wearily. 'You want a casual affair and I don't, so it's easy to settle. We just stop seeing each other.'

'No!' His face was intent, ruthless, filled with the kind of excitement and relentless drive that it showed in pursuit of a major business deal. 'I'm not willing to stop seeing you. Look, we'll play it your way.'

'W-what do you mean?' asked Holly suspiciously, backing away from him.

He followed her and seized her hands.

'Tell me what you want,' he urged. 'You want to be friends with me? A hands-off policy? Just good old-fashioned friendship while we get to know each other? Come on, honey, I don't want to give you up.'

A tremor of misgiving swept through Holly. She thought of the wolf in the old fairy-tales disguised as a harmless sheep. But then she looked into Simon's searing blue eyes and choked back a groan. She didn't want to give him up either.

'How do I know you aren't just spinning me a line?' she demanded warily.

'I guess you'll just have to trust me.'

'But Virginia——'

Simon swore softly under his breath.

'Forget Virginia. She's nothing to do with us. Now come on. Are we going to be friends?'

Holly hesitated. Was she being conned? But Simon was smiling at her so warmly that her doubts melted.

'OK,' she said. 'It's a deal.'

A gleam of triumph lurked in Simon's eyes.

'Good,' he said huskily. 'Well, do you think you'd feel safe enough to come and eat some dessert with me? Now that I have my new hands-off policy?'

Holly rolled her eyes, but joined him at the table. As she sat watching him score an orange into quarters and peel off the segments of skin, she was conscious of a mysterious, aching sense of joy deep inside her. I'm happy, she thought wonderingly. For the first time in months I'm happy. And I really believe that Simon is sincere. That this friendship might grow into something marvellous. Incredibly marvellous.

She had never known before that eating an orange could be a sensual experience, but as she chewed the sweet, pulpy fruit and let it slide down her throat, she was aware of an extraordinary magic about this evening. A magic that seemed to extend to everything around her. The humble, lamplit cabin, the roar of the storm, the lingering warmth of Simon's glances all combined to make her feel transfigured. I've never felt so happy in my life, she thought with a sense of shock. I wonder if it will always be like this between us?

It was shortly after dawn the following morning when Holly was awoken by Paul's return to the cabin. Fortunately he didn't seem in the least bit disconcerted by finding her in his bed, but burst into a rumble of laughter after hearing her disjointed explanation, and backed out of the room. When she came downstairs a few minutes later, she was met by the smell of frying bacon and the sound of murmuring voices. Feeling an unaccustomed shyness, she made her way into the kitchen. After the conversation of the previous evening, she wasn't sure how Simon would behave towards her.

But the warmth in his eyes was unmistakable when he turned to greet her.

'So? Caught out in the rain like a pair of rats, were you?' boomed Paul jovially. 'Well, I'm only sorry I've got such a measly breakfast to offer you. But bring your young lady out to stay for a weekend some time, Simon, and I'll see you're both properly fed.'

Holly opened her mouth to protest that she wasn't Simon's young lady and then changed her mind. Blushing, she gave both men a shy, darting smile and sat down on the chair Paul was holding out for her. In spite of his apologies, it was a magnificent breakfast. Bacon, eggs, sausages, hash-brown potatoes, a pitcher of orange juice, and a pot of dense, fragrant black coffee. While they ate, Paul told them how he had spent the evening in a new jazz club in Baton Rouge and stayed overnight. Only when a leisurely hour or so had been spent talking and eating did he get out the keys to his pick-up truck and offer to drive them back to the paddlesteamer.

'I hope you won't hit me over the head with a frying-pan when I tell you this,' said Simon as Paul set them out at the levée by the river. 'But I do have some pretty important correspondence I have to work on with my secretary today.'

Holly pulled a face.

'Well, I'll let you off just this once,' she grumbled. 'But when we get back to New Orleans, I want some time alone with you without any work.'

'It's a deal,' promised Simon.

Throughout the day, Holly felt as if she were walking on air. Nobody made a fuss about their overnight absence and the cooking was easy enough for her to manage with a minimum of effort. The musicians and cameramen had gone off on another photographic expedition, the crew were having a day's shore leave, Simon and his secretary were shut up in his office and the only niggling worry that disturbed her tranquillity was Virginia Cox. When Simon mentioned casually at dinner that he and Holly had spent the night at Paul's house, Holly felt sure that she saw a flash of annoyance in the other woman's eyes but she told herself that she was just being absurd. All the same, she could not shake off the sense of uneasiness that settled on her. I'll be glad when I get back to New Orleans and I can really be alone with Simon, she thought. But even that thought did not bring her much comfort. How was she ever going to find the time to be alone with Simon? With a restaurant to run and a child to look after it wouldn't be easy.

Her spirits lifted somewhat when Simon complimented her on the dinner and then plunged when he told her he'd be working until midnight. Pensively, Holly cleaned up the galley and retired early to her cabin. This was one of the guest suites on the second deck and was just as lavishly appointed as the staterooms that Simon and Virginia were occupying. Yet as she took a shower in the marble-lined bathroom and later padded around on the thick, soft carpet in her bedroom, Holly's lips twisted in a wistful smile. I'd gladly give up the luxury for a bit more of his company she thought. Moodily, she dried her hair and then rummaged in her overnight bag for a pair of cheap, cotton pyjamas. Once she had pulled these on she stared at herself critically in the mirror and a tremor of doubt went through her. No, she just looked ordinary. Plain ordinary. Wild ginger hair, a snub nose, a wide, quirky mouth, freckly skin and not a hint of height or elegance. In fact to tell the truth she was just plain dumpy. So what did Simon see in her? Did he really see anything in her? And then the memory of the way he had looked at her in the cabin came back in a flash and she felt certain that he did. But did he only want her physically or was there more to it than that? In spite of Simon's horror of emotional involvement, was he beginning to care for her at least a little bit?

Sighing, she made her way back into the bedroom, flung all the expensively upholstered cushions on to the floor, drew back the silky, apricot quilted cover and climbed into bed. Propping a pile of pillows against the rosewood headboard, she picked up a novel and tried to read. But after she had read five pages without absorbing a single word, she flung the book down on the floor with the cushions. Linking her hands behind her head, she leaned back against the pillows and began to daydream about Simon. The fluttering excitement that rose inside her at the mere thought of him made her realise how deeply he held her spellbound. I could easily fall in love with him, she thought. Very, very easily. With a quiver of apprehension, she wondered whether she was already in love with him. Careful, Holly, careful, she warned herself. All you agreed to was a friendship. Nothing more. Yet her imagination was too rash and adventurous to be satisfied with that. It flew off on wings to a distant future where Simon had shed all the bitter legacies of his youth and looked at her with love blazing in his eyes. Groaning, she turned over and tried unsuccessfully to blot out the vision.

Well, if anything did come of this rather unlikely relationship, some things would have to change. They would have to find more ways of being together. Simon would have to work less and she would have to... what? Until Heather recovered, she was quite simply locked in. Oh, she might be able to snatch an odd evening to be alone with Simon, find a babysitter or a substitute chef now and then, but you couldn't really build a relationship on that, could you? Although perhaps when Heather was better... What if she sold the restaurant and they went into a catering business together? Just doing lunches, perhaps? Then Heather could have more time with Amber and Holly could see Simon whenever she wanted to... She yawned, snuggled deeper into the pillows and fell into a doze.

It was after midnight when she awoke to find that the light was still on. Annoyed with herself, she blinked and got out of bed to switch it off. But then she wanted a drink of water and after the water she no longer felt sleepy. She wondered what had woken her and then suddenly became aware that the ship's engines were going and the paddle-wheels were churning. It must be pretty out on deck with the whole boat lit up like a Christmas tree and the moon shimmering through the black night. Maybe she ought to go and have a walk and get a breath of fresh air. Perhaps that would put her back to sleep. Pulling on a thin robe, she crept softly out of her room. As she stepped out on to the deck, Holly thought she saw a flicker of shadow cross the moonlight at the far end.

'Who's there?' she called. But there was no answer.

Deciding she had imagined it, she took a couple of steps to the railing and gazed out over the river. It was breathtakingly beautiful. The moon spilt a path of milky white radiance over the dark waters, a warm breeze fanned her cheeks, the elusive scents of trees and swamp grass wafted from the unseen banks and there was no sound but the rhythmic churning of the paddle-wheel hitting the water and sending a great white avalanche of spray cascading through the darkness. Holly rested her elbows on the railing, and stared out at the river. Near the distant bank, another paddlesteamer was forging steadily upstream, its bright lights sending rippling reflections dancing over the dark water. Straining her ears, Holly heard the muted sounds of jazz and the babble of laughter and upraised voices. Then gradually the noise faded into the distance and she was alone again. She smiled, feeling suddenly grateful to Simon for giving her this chance to see the heartland of Louisiana. All her life she had dreamed of riding on a paddlesteamer and now at least one of her ambitions was satisfied.

'Holly?'

She spun round with a gasp. It was Simon, dressed like herself in thin pyjamas and a lightweight robe. His hand rested briefly on her shoulder and without pausing to think, she nestled into the crook of his arm.

'Hey! Are you sure this is permitted?' he demanded. 'What about our new hands-off policy?'

Holly gave a soft gurgle of laughter and nestled closer into his hold.

'Yes, it's permitted,' she assured him. 'Besides, I'm starting to think the hands-off policy could be slowly relaxed.'

'I'm glad to hear it, and I certainly can't waste an opportunity like that,' replied Simon, moving adroitly to put both of his hands down on the railing so that she was trapped in front of him.

And yet she felt totally safe. In fact, it felt wonderful to have that warm, masculine body clasped so protectively around her. She shut her eyes, glorying in his nearness, inhaling the wild, spicy masculine scent of his body, yearning for an even closer union. He made a low sound deep in his throat and leaned forward, burying his face in her hair.

'You're gorgeous, Holly,' he said. 'Do you know that?'

'Don't be silly,' she protested self-consciously. 'How can I be gorgeous? I'm just ordinary. No special talents apart from cooking, zillions of freckles and I'm too plump.'

Simon gave a soft growl of laughter. 'Don't put yourself down like that,' he told her. 'I don't think you're ordinary. I think you're extraordinarily wise, extraordinarily generous and extraordinarily desirable. No, cancel the last one.'

'Why?' demanded Holly, feeling rather offended. 'Don't you think I am desirable?'

'Yes, I do,' Simon assured her. 'But I'm not allowed to say it, am I?'

She giggled again.

'Well, I guess it's OK if you just think it,' she said.

Simon's voice suddenly took on a serious note. He drew her closer to him, and bending his neck, imprinted a trail of feather-light kisses on her warm hair.

'I do think it,' he whispered. 'And I think you should stick around in New Orleans as long as possible... Kiss me, Holly.'

She wasn't sure whether it was a command or a request and it never occurred to her to refuse, because she realised now that she wanted this more than anything on earth. As his powerful arms tightened around her and his warm mouth came down on hers, she gave a soft gasp of delight and moved hesitantly to meet him. His kisses were deep, wild and infinitely thrilling. But they were also indescribably tormenting. Arching her back, she gave a low whimper as he caught her hard against him. Through their thin clothes she could feel the heat of his body coming off in waves, hear the thudding of his heart, and sense the violent arousal which he was struggling to contain. With a savage muttering he thrust her suddenly away from him, as if casting temptation away.

'No,' he muttered hoarsely. 'It's too soon. I'll wait until you're ready. But it will come, won't it, you sensual little witch?'

A strange, fluttering sensation woke inside her and she found it suddenly difficult to breathe. In that moment she did not, could not believe that Simon was driven only by the selfish pursuit of his own pleasures. He must feel something for her. He must. He must! He couldn't be just spinning her a line in a callous attempt to seduce her, she was certain of it. Swallowing hard, she nodded.

'Yes,' she said huskily, and moved closer to him so that once again she was standing with her head nestled against his shoulder, no longer in a passionate embrace, but warm, close, tender. Then suddenly a faint sound like a stealthy footstep caught her attention. She whirled around.

'What was that?' she demanded in alarm.

'What was what?' Simon asked in a puzzled voice.

'I thought I heard something,' she said, her heart pounding against her ribs.

'Don't be silly, darling. You're jumping at shadows.'

Darling. She hugged the word to her, exulting in it. Simon smiled down at her rather pensively and drew his forefinger in a playful trail down her cheek.

'Well, if I'm going to keep my sanity, I think it's time we went off to our separate beds,' he growled. 'But when we get back to New Orleans, I want to see a lot of you, Holly. Promise?'

'Promise,' she agreed.

Putting his arm around her shoulders, he led her back inside the ship and escorted her to the door of the cabin where he kissed her lightly on the cheek and then tilted her chin up so that he could gaze into her eyes. A current of warmth and longing and strange expectancy seemed to flow between them and then Simon backed reluctantly away.

'Goodnight,' he said.

At five-thirty the next morning, Holly sprang into life, yawning and blinking, at the shrill summons of her alarm clock. With a groan she sat up. Well, if she and Simon ever did get married, one thing she would have to break him of was this barbarous habit of a cooked breakfast, at a time when even self-respecting roosters were still snoring on their queen-size ensembles. But after a hasty sprinkle in the shower she pulled on shorts and a T-shirt and made her way down to the galley. Ten minutes later, she came back upstairs with the tray and went into the tiny pantry to make Simon's coffee. She was just coming back out again when the door of Simon's cabin opened and a figure came tiptoeing out. And it was then that

Holly had the nastiest shock that she had ever experienced in her life. It was so horrifying that she almost dropped the tray.

'Virginia,' she breathed.

Yes, it was Virginia. But not Virginia as Holly had ever seen her before. Not Virginia with the severely combed hair and the tortoiseshell glasses, the almost military embodiment of precision and efficiency. This Virginia was barely recognisable. She was wearing peach-coloured satin pyjamas with the top button undone, her blonde hair was tumbled in an unruly mass around her shoulders and she wore the slumbrous, self-satisfied expression of a cat who had been at the cream. Suddenly she seemed to become aware of Holly. She started and attempted to tidy her hair, furtively buttoning her pyjamas with her free hand.

'Oh,' she said in a flustered voice. 'I didn't expect you to be up this early.'

Holly stared at her blindly. The implications of what she had just seen were beginning to sink in and a bitter, twisting misery seemed to be clenching her insides. She held her breath, not willing to subject herself to the humiliation of dropping the tray and running blindly for cover.

'I—I had to take—Simon's breakfast,' she stammered.

'Oh, give it to me, I'll take it in to him,' said Virginia, taking the tray out of her nerveless hands. 'He's in the shower right now, so it's probably better if you don't go in. I wouldn't want you to be embarrassed.'

And she gave Holly another small, feline smile and vanished with the tray. Embarrassed! thought Holly almost hysterically, making her way into the nearest shelter, which happened to be the pantry. How could I be any more embarrassed than I already am? To know that Simon was kissing me on the deck last night, and then spent the night with her! Isn't that embarrassing enough? A dry sob rose in her throat and, simply in order to have something to do, she poured herself a cup of coffee. But her hands were shaking so much that the percolator clattered against the cup and half the coffee spilled in the saucer. She was still staring blindly down at the black liquid when there was a light tap at the pantry door and Virginia came in. In spite of the peach pyjamas, she had recovered her usual aura of efficiency and Holly was seized by a strange feeling of unreality as she looked at her.

'What is it? Do you want me to cook you some breakfast?' she asked in a dazed voice.

'No, I'm not hungry, thanks. I thought you and I should have a little talk.'

'Talk?' demanded Holly in alarm. 'What is there to talk about?'

'Well, Simon of course,' purred Virginia. 'You mustn't be so offended by what you saw, Holly. After all, it's only natural that Simon and I should be sleeping together. We are getting married in a few weeks' time, you know.'

Holly felt as shocked and winded as if somebody had just punched her in the stomach. For a moment her entire body seemed frozen, then the first blazing brand of suspicion began to crackle through her, warming her back into life. She stared at Virginia in horror and disbelief.

'I don't believe you,' she said flatly. 'This is all some kind of trick.'

Virginia sighed and raised her eyebrows.

'You poor girl,' she murmured. 'You've really got a crush on Simon, haven't you? But you're wasting your time, you know. He's going to marry me.'

'Oh, is he?' retorted Holly. 'Well, that's easy to check! I'll just go and ask him.'

'Don't be a fool,' snapped Virginia. 'You'll only make yourself look ridiculous. Simon may have been playing around with you on the side—men are like that—but he's marrying me in August and that's the truth.'

'Prove it,' challenged Holly.

Virginia smirked.

'How very undignified you are, my dear,' she sighed wearily. 'But if nothing else will satisfy you, all right, you'll have your proof. Come with me.'

Too shattered to argue, Holly followed her into her cabin. Virginia took out a leather notecase and extracted a single sheet of paper which she held out to Holly.

'I assume you recognise Simon's handwriting,' she said. 'Or aren't you well enough acquainted with him for that? Still it'll be easy enough for you to check up on later. This is a letter he wrote to me last summer. Forgive me if I don't show you the first page, it's rather... personal. But this should be enough to convince you.'

Feeling numb with horror, Holly looked down at the single sheet of paper she held in her hands and began mechanically to read. It was awful. The words blurred before her eyes and then cleared again. She didn't want to believe what she was seeing. And yet she could not deny that the neat, calligraphy was really Simon's or even that the deadly words it contained were his. Blinking hard, she stared down at what it said.

> 'I'm in love with you, Virginia, and I don't believe my feelings will ever change. I know your career is important to you, but I think marriage may be the best thing for both of us. If you're still of the same mind when you come next summer, why don't we tie the knot in August so that you can move house before the fall semester? My mother sends her regards and she's delighted at the thought of having you as a daughter-in-law. Write soon and let me know your plans.
> Simon.

Virginia was watching her, with a small triumphant smile lurking around the corners of her lips.

'Well? Convinced?' she demanded, reaching out her hand for the letter.

Holly felt as if an abyss had just opened up at her feet and she had fallen into it. Too dazed and shaken to comprehend what had really happened, she only knew that she was more deeply hurt than she had ever been in her life. And yet for all her pain and anger, she still managed to summon a pathetic dignity.

'I hope you'll both be very happy,' she said tonelessly.

And then she bolted for the door. There was no doubt in her mind now. All her bright dreams were over. Simon Madigan had betrayed her trust.

CHAPTER NINE

THE next few hours passed in a dismal blur for Holly. Somehow she managed to cook breakfast for the crew and the other passengers but she had no idea what she put on the table in front of them and by ten o'clock in the morning, when the paddlesteamer docked in New Orleans, she felt as dazed and disoriented as a sleepwalker. Appropriately enough, the weather was dismal so that the city was hidden behind a curtain of grey, driving rain. Desperate to avoid any more encounters with Simon, Holly had her small overnight bag packed and ready and the moment they drew up beside the levée, she was the first up the gangplank. Without a backward look, she vanished into the rain in search of a taxi. Ten minutes later she arrived at Heather's apartment, her clothes soaked and her throat aching with unshed tears. A note stuck in the front door announced that her neighbour had taken Amber to the park, so Holly had no reason even to keep up a pretence of cheerfulness. But it wasn't in her nature to sit around feeling sorry for herself.

Determined not to give way to her unhappiness, she set herself the worst job she could think of, which was to clean out the oven. But not long after, when she was kneeling on a folded newspaper, wearing a pair of blackened rubber gloves, and choking at the acrid fumes from the cleaner, the telephone suddenly rang. Holly felt a sense of impending dread, as if she had just stepped into the path of an oncoming truck. Her heart raced and her skin felt clammy. For a moment she thought of letting the phone ring and ring without answering it, but she couldn't bring herself to do it. It might be an emergency, something to do with Amber or Heather. Or it might be urgent news about the restaurant. Peeling off the rubber gloves, she stalked across the room and picked up the receiver as gingerly as if it were a spider.

'Hello?' she said huskily.

'Holly,' it was his voice. Deep, vibrant, unmistakably exasperated. 'Why the hell did you run off like that? I was hoping we could have lunch together.'

Her throat tightened agonisingly.

'I can't——' she began.

'Well, I can't either, now. I've just had a phone call from Europe about a major hitch in my distribution over there. I'll have to fly to Frankfurt and sort it out. If it's as bad as I think, I'll probably be gone for a couple of weeks, but I'll be in touch with you as soon as I get back.'

Holly tried to speak and failed. Her throat felt as raw and scraped as if she had a bad cold. Then suddenly she found her voice.

'No!' she exclaimed hoarsely. 'I don't want to see you, Simon. It was all a mistake. I don't want a casual affair with you. Or even a friendship. There are other people involved and someone's going to get hurt. It's better if we don't meet again.'

'Why should anyone get hurt? What are you talking about, Holly?'

She drew in a long, shuddering breath.

'Don't ask me to spell it out, Simon. I can't bear it. I wish I'd never let you touch me. Now please, please get out of my life!'

And she slammed down the phone, only to pick it up immediately and leave it off the hook. This time she was far too agitated to worry that anyone else might try and contact her. Anyway, it wouldn't be for long. Hadn't he said he was catching the three o'clock plane on his way to Europe? Well, she could count on one thing. Simon

Madigan would never miss a meeting as important as that for the sake of an affair with a mere kitchenmaid! Once three o'clock had passed, she would be safe. At least for the next two weeks. And then perhaps a miracle would happen, and she could leave New Orleans and never see him again.

But unfortunately, miracles were as scarce as ever during the next two weeks. The plumber and tiler still didn't come to do the repairs at the restaurant, the local government authority sent out another letter threatening closure and the air-conditioning in the restaurant needed major surgery. The only good news was that Heather seemed to be making an unexpectedly swift recovery and was likely to be out of hospital sooner than expected. However, it would be many more weeks before she was fit to work again and her parents had written again, urging her to bring Amber to Hawaii for a holiday and convalescence. It looked as if Holly would have to stay in New Orleans if the embattled restaurant was to avoid closure.

'I can't ask you to do it, Holly,' said Heather the day before she was due to come out of hospital. 'It's not fair to you. Maybe it would be best if I just sold the place anyway.'

'Oh, don't be ridiculous,' cried Holly impatiently. 'If you want to sell it when you're well again, that's fine. But don't make the decision just because you're afraid I can't cope. I love New Orleans. I'm having a great time.'

It would have been true if it hadn't been for the fiasco of her involvement with Simon. It was a wonderful city, vibrant, beautiful and full of life. But Holly hadn't told her sister of the traumatic love affair which had robbed the city of all its charm. For one thing, she didn't want to worry Heather. And for another thing, she didn't want to hear her moaning like a Greek chorus about how she had always predicted disaster. No, the truth was that

Holly was stuck. She would have to stay at La Crevette and just hope that Simon had the decency to stay away from her. A vain hope.

The next morning was the big day when Heather was due to come out of hospital. In the morning, Holly got up early and took her niece Amber to the big market on Decatur Street to buy some flowers and sweets to celebrate the occasion. As they strolled around, Holly was acutely aware of the fact that Simon must now be back in the city and absurdly, she kept expecting him to leap out at any moment from behind the biscuit-coloured Doric columns that supported the long building. But after a while, the soothing charm of the place began to work its spell on her and she relaxed enough to enjoy walking through the long colonnades. Under the shelter of the roof there was a welcome shade and the air was filled with an exciting mixture of scents. Amber pranced along, yelping like a puppy and darting off to investigate every new feature.

'What are those things hanging from the roof beams, Aunt Holly? Are they onions? Garlic? Yuck! Can I have some pears? Please, please. Why don't you buy a pineapple? Oh, look, what a pretty hat! Well, I didn't mean to step in it. I don't think people should leave squashed bananas on the floor, do you?'

By the time they reached the second building, Holly was feeling about eighty years old and badly in need of admission to a rest-home.

'Why don't you choose some flowers for your Mommy?' she suggested. 'And then we'll go home and have a nice cup of coffee and put our feet up.'

'All right,' agreed Amber gleefully. 'Can we have those white ones? The really big ones that smell nice? And can I do paintings and stick them up all over the living-room to give Mommy a nice surprise?'

'Sure, honey. Anything. Anything.'

The stall holder smiled down indulgently at Amber's dancing eyes and bobbing ginger topknot as she handed over the bunch of damp, scented, white lilies.

'Your little girl sure does look like you, ma'am,' she commented.

'Oh, she's not my——' began Holly and then her heart knocked so sharply against her ribs that it shocked her. For her worst fantasies were suddenly being realised. Halfway down the concourse, Simon Madigan had just stepped out from between two stalls and was threading his way purposefully towards them. Holly stared at him in consternation and looked wildly around for an escape route. But short of grabbing Amber by the hand and taking to their heels, there was nothing she could do. Amber pressed her clenched fist against her mouth and gave an explosive fizz of laughter.

'That lady thought you were my Mommy,' she said. 'Isn't that funny?'

A wild inspiration suddenly seized Holly. Crouching down beside her niece she whispered into her ear.

'Listen, Amber. See that man coming towards us? When he stops to talk to us, I want you to pretend that I am your Mommy. OK?'

Amber wrinkled her freckled nose in bewilderment.

'Is it a game?' she demanded doubtfully.

'Yes, sweetheart. It's a game,' whispered Holly hastily and then she rose to her feet.

In spite of all her antagonism towards Simon, Holly could not prevent a wave of yearning sweeping through her at the sight of that lean, dark unsmiling figure striding towards her. He came to a halt and stood staring at her with his hands on his hips and an expression of intense, hungry longing on his face.

'Your neighbour told me you were here,' he said without a word of greeting. 'I've missed you.'

Holly felt an imbecilic urge to stammer, 'I've missed you, too,' but she bit back the words. Dragging her gaze away from him, she nudged Amber. The little girl jumped.

'Shouldn't we be going home now, Mommy?' she recited in a singsong voice.

For the first time Simon seemed to become aware of the child. His gaze flew down to her, shot back up to Holly's face and then came to a halt. An appalled expression spread over his features.

'Is this why you didn't want to get involved with me?' he demanded in a low rapid voice.

'Yes,' faltered Holly.

'You're married?'

'No.'

The swift monosyllable was out before she even had time to lie. Her eyes met his in silent anguish and she flushed crimson, suddenly ashamed of herself for this ridiculous deception, and yet still tormented by her inability to tell him the truth. How could she discuss the whole, tangled saga of Virginia here in this public place, in front of her niece, in front of all these people? She would simply break down and howl if she tried. Instead, she stood and stared at him in wretched silence. He looked down at the little girl again, and a faint, bitter smile twisted his lips.

'Why didn't you trust me enough to tell me?' he demanded.

'Does it even matter?' Belatedly, Holly gathered her wits. Snatching Amber's hand, she headed for the nearest gap in the portico. 'Look, we've got to go.'

Simon strode rapidly after her and caught her up near a line of horse-drawn surreys outside the building.

'Holly, wait,' he urged. 'It's a hell of shock, but give me time to get used to it. She's a cute kid and we'll get to like each other. Anyway, you're wasting your time running out on me. I still intend to have you, Holly!'

'No!'

Holly's voice was little more than a frozen whisper. Grabbing Amber's arm, she hoisted her into the back of a surrey and climbed up beside her.

'Robespierre Street, please, and hurry,' she said to the driver.

The horse's hooves began to clop smartly along the road and Simon had to run to keep up with the vehicle. He could have easily leapt into it before it gained speed, but he didn't. Instead, he stretched out one hand to her in a gesture of violent reproach.

'Holly, damn you, stop!'

'No.'

As they broke away from the market area and into the maze of streets of the French Quarter, Holly slumped back against the leather seats and gave a choking groan. For a moment she wondered whether there had been some appalling mistake. Simon had looked furious. Utterly furious. And yet for an instant she had glimpsed something else in his eyes. Some unreadable emotion that might have been a burning desire to crush her in his arms rather than to wring her neck. Was it remotely possible that he really did love her? He wouldn't go to such lengths just to pursue a meaningless secret love affair, would he? And he couldn't honestly be planning to marry Virginia if he could speak to Holly with such passionate intensity in his voice. Could he? An agonised sense of uncertainty gripped her and she actually leaned forward towards the driver. There must be some mistake, there must be! She would ask him to drive her back to the market. She would find Simon and insist on an explanation!

'Excuse me?'

'Yes, ma'am?'

Then Holly thought of the letter. That hateful, implacable document that set down the truth in black and white. 'I'm in love with you, Virginia, and I don't belive my feelings will ever change...' With a faint, defeated gasp she sank back in her place.

'Nothing,' she said dully. 'I'm sorry to trouble you.'

Although she didn't cry, her distress was obvious even to a five-year-old. Amber knelt on the seat beside her and put her arms around Holly's neck with a worried expression.

'What's the matter, Aunt Holly?' she asked. 'Didn't you enjoy playing that game?'

It was another three days before she saw Simon and they were three of the most miserable, dreary days in Holly's life. Once she had seen Heather and Amber off at the airport, there wasn't even the remedy of constant business to numb her pain. Working in the restaurant kept her busy from three o'clock in the afternoon until after midnight, but there were still the broken nights spent tossing and turning and the long, empty mornings to fill. She could have gone sightseeing, but she no longer had the heart for that. All the features of New Orleans which had fascinated her when she first arrived now seemed flat and lifeless. She plodded through the French Quarter with her head down, not even noticing the ornate iron gas-lamps, the beautiful old houses, the gracious spires of the St Louis Cathedral. She sat in coffee shops and slowly chewed beignets without really tasting the crisp, sugar-dusted doughnuts, she walked past street musicians with trumpets and clarinets but did not pause to listen, and when she moved among the stalls of brightly coloured fruit and vegetables of the French market in the mornings, she felt like a sleepwalker. It was as if some vital organ had been removed from her body, leaving her with nothing but a mysterious ache. She tried to cheer herself up by planning what she would do next, but that only made her feel worse.

Of course, there was nothing much she could do, until Heather returned from Hawaii and made a decision about the restaurant's future. But once that happened, Holly would be free. Free to do what? she wondered gloomily. I could go to Hawaii or Sydney, and work in a big hotel. Or I could even go to Europe and get a job as a chef cruising around the Mediterranean with some Arab billionaire. But all of these choices filled her with a leaden sense of dismay. In the past she had always loved travelling, had rejoiced at the chance to hop on a plane and go to a new country, but now... I want to stay here, she thought unhappily. So I can be near him. Even if I can't see him, at least I'll know he's close by. The realisation appalled her. When Dennis had left her, she had been grimly relieved that an ocean and an entire continent separated her from him, had dreaded the thought that she might have to see him again, or even breathe the same air as him, but with Simon it was different. However much he had hurt her, she knew in her innermost heart that she hungered for a glimpse of him.

Yet that didn't stop her from going into a tailspin of panic when he appeared at the restaurant. It was a Friday evening shortly after eight o'clock and the place was already humming with life. To save on costs, Holly didn't employ a waiter. The tiny dining-room would only seat twenty guests, so with Sophie in the kitchen and Sophie's husband Joel playing the piano, Holly did all the waiting on the tables herself. And whenever there was a quiet moment she would fly back to the kitchen to help Sophie. On this particular Friday evening, the restaurant was busier than ever. Nearly all the tables were full, and the babble from the people competed with the noises from the street outside and the catchy ragtime tunes that Joel was playing on the piano. Holly stood with her back to the door and a notebook in her hands as she scrawled down an order for a table of eight.

'Right. So that's French bread for everybody, chicken and sausage gumbo for three, stuffed bell peppers for one, shrimp Creole as the first course for three and nothing for the lady on the left. Now, how about a main course?'

'Excuse me, ma'am,' said one of the diners. 'But there's a guy waiting at the front desk. And he looks real steamed up about something.'

Holly's skin rose in goosebumps and she turned slowly. But there could be no mistake. It was Simon. Lean, dark, casually dressed and unmistakably smouldering. His unwinking blue eyes met hers across the crowded room and she felt a panic-stricken urge to bolt for cover. But Simon gave her a faint, forbidding shake of his head. Apart from the way his fingers were drumming on the reception desk, there was no sign that there was anything amiss. And yet Holly felt a sense of danger as ominous as if she were awaiting the onslaught of a tidal wave or some cataclysmic nuclear explosion.

'No hurry, ma'am,' he said in a courteous voice, as if she really were just a waitress. 'Please deal with your other customers first. I'm just waiting for a table. And I'm happy to wait till midnight if necessary.'

Holly shuddered. Her mouth felt suddenly dry and her pulses were racing. Hastily she scrawled down the rest of the order, gave the people a feeble smile and then threaded her way through the tables to Simon.

'What are you doing here?' she demanded under her breath.

He smiled at her. A hard, wolfish smile.

'I've come for dinner. Surely you're not going to throw out a paying customer?'

She stared at him in horror.

'You can't,' she gabbled. 'We're full.'

'What about that table by the window? That's empty.'

'It's reserved.'

'There's no sign on it. Anyway, I'm taking it. You can throw me out, Holly. If you dare.'

With a silent inward groan, she could do nothing but watch helplessly as he shouldered his way through the tables to the empty seat.

'I'll have a hurricane punch to drink,' he announced. 'A bowl of seafood jambalaya with a salad and, for dessert, your speciality. The butter pecan cheesecake.'

Horrified, Holly gazed wildly around her for some means of escape from this ridiculous situation. But what could she do? She couldn't cause a scene by insisting on throwing Simon out for no apparent reason. After all, it wasn't as though he was drunk or being abusive. And the other customers in the restaurant had accepted his arrival without the slightest flicker of attention. No, she would simply have to serve him, and hope he left soon. Casting him a furious glance, she brought her notebook back out of her apron pocket and made a few hasty notes.

'Very good, sir,' she murmured.

'That's what I like to see,' he murmured approvingly. 'Somebody respectful waiting on me. By the way, Holly, how's your... daughter?'

Holly winced. He knows, she thought frantically. He's found out that I lied to him. Or has he? Perhaps it's only a polite enquiry. And then Simon's lips twisted into a bitter smile that left her in no doubt at all.

'Or should I say your niece?' he added.

Muttering something incoherent, Holly fled to the kitchen. Somehow she managed to deliver the order for both tables to Sophie, then she hastily crammed eight substantial hunks of French bread into a wicker basket and took it out to the dining-room. After that, she made up Simon's hurricane punch. But as she set down the tall, festive-looking glass full of red liquid adorned with ice, a cherry and a straw, her hand was shaking slightly.

'No need to be nervous, Holly,' said Simon in velvety tones. 'I'm not going to make a scene here in the restaurant. I intend to wait until we're all alone together to discuss our problems.'

That news only made Holly more nervous than ever and as the time flew by she was acutely conscious of the way Simon's eyes followed her around the room. Usually she enjoyed the atmosphere of the small restaurant, with its soft candlelight, pumpkin-coloured walls and potted palms casting strange, jungly shadows. The hum of conversation, the bursts of laughter, the loud, catchy ragtime music that Joel pounded out of the piano had always lifted her spirits, but not tonight. Tonight she was conscious only of a desperately mounting tension, a growing sense of apprehension and a wish to escape. Would there never come an end to the way Simon sat there brooding silently, his eyes following her every movement?

It did finish, but not in the way Holly expected. At ten o'clock, as always, Joel left the piano for a short break and a cold drink. But, as the elderly black man was shuffling out between the piano and the front desk in the direction of the kitchen, a guest called a question from the far side of the room.

'Pardon me, sir?' demanded Joel, cupping his hand to his ear.

'I said, do you know any piano pieces like Art Tatum used to play?'

His eyes still fixed attentively on the guest as if he were trying to lipread, Joel moved a couple of paces further forward.

'I'm sorry, sir, I still can't——'

His last words were lost, for suddenly, Joel caught his foot in the gap between the tiles, stumbled and fell heavily on the floor. With a startled shriek, Holly ran to him, and fell on her knees beside him.

'Oh, Joel, I'm so sorry,' she cried. 'Are you hurt? It's all my fault, I should have had that fixed ages ago.'

Joel sat up, looking rather shaken.

'Now, don't you take on, honey,' he warned. 'I ain't dead yet. It's just my... back.'

Holly sensed a large, masculine presence behind her and was relieved to find Simon kneeling on Joel's other side. With brisk efficiency, he checked the old man's limbs, and then hoisting him to his feet, helped him hobble into the kitchen, where Joel sank gratefully into a chair.

'I'm sorry, sugar,' said the old man, shaking his head. 'I ain't badly hurt, but I done put my back out again. I won't be able to play that piano any more tonight, that's for sure.'

'Poor Joel, I'm so sorry,' cried Holly in an anxious voice. 'I do hope you haven't hurt yourself seriously. I think you should see a doctor, just in case.'

'I'll take him,' offered Simon instantly.

'Oh, would you?' cried Holly gratefully. 'I'd be glad to pay.'

'Don't be so darned foolish!' growled Simon, waving her off as she grabbed her handbag. 'Is there anything you need to take with you, Joel?'

'No, sir.'

But Holly darted into the restaurant and came back with a bottle of bourbon.

'Take this and have a drink to cheer yourself up,' she suggested wryly. 'It's probably nicer than aspirin.'

Joel winked at her.

'It sure is,' he agreed.

Holly felt dreadful after the door closed on their departing backs. She was convinced that the accident was her fault and said as much to Sophie. But Sophie urged her not to talk foolishness.

'He could've put his back out just as easily at home, ma'am, and you know it. In fact, he often does. It's just bad luck and that's the truth. But we got too much work to do to stand here worrying about it. Now you go take this chicken and sausage gumbo out before it gets cold.'

It was a great relief an hour later when Simon returned with the news that Joel was not badly hurt.

'The doctor says that he'll need three or four days' rest,' he announced. 'But there's nothing broken. And no serious harm done.'

Holly let out a ragged sigh.

'Well, thank goodness for that,' she said. 'You're sure he's all right, Simon?'

Simon nodded.

'The only thing that's worrying Joel is who's going to play the piano till closing time tonight,' he said. 'He told me it's one of your busiest nights and people come in for the live music.'

'Well, that's true,' agreed Holly. 'But they'll just have to put up with cassette tapes for the rest of the evening.'

Simon stroked his chin thoughtfully.

'You know, I could do better than that,' he offered. 'I'm a pretty mean jazz pianist myself.'

Holly stared at him in bewilderment.

'What?' she demanded.

Simon gave a low growl of laughter.

'I can tickle the old ivories with the best of them,' he announced. 'I'll be glad to play for you if you like. It will fill up a rather boring evening. Just listen.'

And listen she did. Simon strolled out to the piano, opened the lid and sat down on the stool. And before Holly's astonished eyes, he underwent a transformation that she would have never believed possible. After a moment's theatrical pause, his fingers slammed down on the keys and a hectic rhythm of notes exploded into the air. Holly listened in disbelief as Simon's fingers flew over the keys. He began with the light syncopation of ragtime and then passed on to a driving beat in which the flattened notes of the blues scale were strongly evident. The melodies were simple, mostly march tunes, but he improvised around them in a freewheeling counterpoint that was dazzling in its virtuosity. One by one the customers laid down their glasses and forks and leaned forward eagerly to listen to the music. When at last it came to an end, there were whistles and shrieks of approval, loud clapping and demands for more. With a sudden start, Holly realised she had done no work at all for ten minutes and dashed hastily into the kitchen.

Throughout the rest of the evening Simon played steadily, ranging over every style of jazz, from the swaggering bravado of swing to the friendly rhythms of beebop, occasionally pausing to sip a hurricane punch or to play a request song for a customer. His face wore a smile, his eyes were lit up and he looked like a man who was thoroughly enjoying himself. Stealing occasional glances at him from the kitchen door, Holly wondered how on earth she had ever thought him rigid and humourless. Here at the piano, he seemed like the man she had known out at Paul's cabin. Relaxed, graceful, full of passion and energy and instinct. An entirely different person from the controlled, ruthlessly efficient businessman whom she had first met. Yet when the restaurant finally closed shortly after two o'clock, when the kitchen had been scrubbed down, the last guest ushered on to the street and Sophie safely put into a taxi, it was the hard-faced businessman who confronted Holly again.

As she took her bag from the hook on the back porch, his hand closed over hers.

'I'll walk you home,' he announced.

'No, thank you,' she replied miserably.

'I'm not asking you, I'm telling you. I'll walk you home.'

'Simon, I don't want anything further to do with you.'

'Oh, no, you don't! You're not wriggling out of it that easily, Holly. If you still want to break up with me after we've talked, that's fine, that's your privilege. But you're not leaving me with so many important questions unanswered. And if we're going to fight, I intend to do it in privacy and comfort. I'm taking you home.'

'Who says we're going to fight?' Holly challenged.

Simon gave her a grim smile.

'I hope we won't,' he replied in a clipped voice. 'But somehow I have a premonition that we will.'

CHAPTER TEN

HOLLY cast him a smouldering glance.

'I hate you,' she flung at him.

He laughed mirthlessly.

'Good, that's a start. Hate and love are two sides of the same coin, you know.'

'Don't flatter yourself,' she snapped.

And yet somehow her heart began to sing at his words. Could this be Simon, who had always been so suspicious of emotions, talking about love as if he wanted her to feel it for him? Of course, that might be just vanity on his part... All the same, she produced the keys and Simon locked up the building before leading her through the courtyard on to the crowded street. Without asking her permission he put his arm through hers and began walking briskly down the centre of the street. She was still furious with him and yet as they walked she realised with a twinge of annoyance that he was right. Love and hate were two sides of the same coin. However angry he had made her, she still felt an unwilling thrill of pleasure in being here beside him, feeling his warm, muscular arm against hers, sensing the way he was adapting his longer stride to her short legs. Even at this late hour there were still quite a few people on the streets, with an occasional vehicle edging past them.

'Shouldn't we be on the sidewalk?' demanded Holly.

'Banquette,' corrected Simon.

'What?'

'Banquette. You said sidewalk. In New Orleans they're called banquettes. You should know that if you're going to stay on here.'

'Who says I'm going to stay on here? Heather will be back in a few weeks to take over the restaurant. I'll be free to leave.'

'Will you?'

When they turned into Robespierre Street, Holly felt her heart beating faster. She couldn't deny that she was apprehensive about the storm that was inevitably brewing with Simon and yet at the same time she had an odd, fluttering sense almost of expectancy or excitement. Maybe he did have some explanation, some perfectly good explanation for the way he had behaved. Maybe it wasn't all over between them. All the same, she made one last-ditch attempt to fend him off when they reached the front door of the apartment.

'I really don't think you should come in,' she babbled. 'I don't think we have anything more to say to each other.'

His answer was brief, violent and forthright. And so rude that it shocked her. With a faint gasp she stood aside unresisting as he stepped into the small hall, closed the front door and went into the living room. He snapped on the overhead light revealing the room in all its shabbiness. Heather had done her best to soften it with masses of potted plants, brightly coloured patchwork cushions, colourful family photos and paintings by Amber on the walls. But nothing could disguise the cracks in the plaster, the threadbare spot in the carpet near the kitchen door or the stuffing that was spilling out of the hole in the brown sofa.

Simon gazed shrewdly around, if as he were taking in every detail. Then he walked deliberately across to Amber's art gallery and unhitched one of the paintings from its mooring of bluetack. It was a portrait captioned in huge letters, 'Aunt Holly.' For a moment he stood gazing grimly down at the riot of orange curls, the smiling mouth full of what appeared to be shark's teeth, the rigidly outstretched arms with seastar fingers and the square shaped body and legs. An unreadable expression came into his eyes and he gazed piercingly at Holly. She squirmed uncomfortably under that disconcerting stare and braced herself for a blistering attack. Yet when he spoke his words were completely unexpected.

'Do you really have a third nostril?' he asked, glancing down at the painting in his hand.

Holly gave a startled gasp of laughter.

'No, of course not. Amber's details are a bit strange sometimes. I don't have ninety-four teeth either.'

'Why did you lie to me about her, Holly?'

His voice was grave, unexpectedly gentle and to her horror Holly found that it brought her close to tears.

'I...she...well, it was impulse really. I wanted something that would get rid of you. Something that would make you realise how impossible it was between us.'

'Impossible? Why? Why is it impossible? All we were talking about was friendship, for heaven's sake! Even so, if Amber had really been your child, I could see why you might have thought it wouldn't work. Maybe she wouldn't have liked me, maybe she would have felt jealous at sharing you with someone else. Maybe you would have been too badly hurt and betrayed by her father to want anything to do with another man. Hell, there are half a dozen different reasons why you might not have wanted to keep seeing me. Pathetic reasons, but understandable. And that's what I really believed was going on until I had the sense to check up on your story.'

'What do you mean, "check up"?' asked Holly sharply. Simon made an impatient gesture with his hands.

'I sent an employee of mine around to make discreet enquiries about you,' he replied.

'Enquiries? How dare you?' retorted Holly.

'Come on, Holly,' snapped Simon. 'What did you expect me to do? Give you up without a fight? I've never in my life given up on anything I wanted. And I want you, Holly. Make no mistake about that. I want you.'

Holly gave a gasp of bitter laughter.

'And how is that supposed to make me feel?' she jeered. 'Grateful? Well, it doesn't, Simon. It makes me feel like an object. A thing. Something you're pursuing the way you pursue a company takeover. Not a human being, not somebody with feelings. And that's been the whole trouble with us, right from the start. You've never thought about my feelings, only about your own. You have no consideration whatsoever!'

'Consideration?' echoed Simon incredulously. 'Consideration? You're a fine one to talk about consideration! How much consideration did you show to me, spinning me a line about how you were an unmarried mother and then running off and leaving me? You want to hear about feelings? I'll tell you about feelings. I feel so furious with you I could wring your goddamn neck!'

Holly's blood boiled with indignation. What was Simon, some kind of human bulldozer? First he thought he could two time her, then have the gall to investigate her private life and finally act as if he were the injured party. What a nerve the man had!

'Oh, I see,' she cried. 'Is that what you're here for?'

'No, it isn't,' snarled Simon.

He took a long, shuddering breath and made an obvious attempt to control his temper but his blue eyes still blazed fire.

'I'm here because I think there's still something between us, Holly, something to save. Something a bit more passionate than just friendship! Look, even if Amber had been your child, I think we could have got over that difficulty. But we don't have to face that problem. So what other obstacle can be big enough to keep us apart?'

Holly ground her teeth.

'Do I have to spell it out to you in words of one syllable?' she choked.

Simon gave a bitter laugh.

'Yes, I guess you do, sweetheart,' he retorted. 'Because I'm just not quick enough on the uptake to see what the problem is. Why don't you want to get involved with me?'

Holly bit hard on her lower lip.

'Because I'm not interested in playing second fiddle,' she said in a rush. 'Because I don't want a cheap and nasty affair on the side, when all the time you're seriously involved with someone else!'

'Seriously involved with someone else?' echoed Simon in a bewildered voice. 'What the hell are you talking about, Holly?'

All Holly's fragile self-control snapped.

'I'm talking about Virginia Cox,' she shouted. 'The woman you're planning to marry!'

There was a moment's shocked silence in which Holly was acutely aware of the violent pounding of her heart and the lump in her throat which threatened to choke her. Well, at least it was out now. The truth. But not the whole truth. For she could never tell Simon what she could scarcely bear to admit to herself. That, however humiliated she felt by his betrayal, however much she hated him, she still felt a deep, physical ache of longing for him, still wanted to rush blindly into his arms and burrow into his embrace. Casting him a tormented glance, she saw a succession of feelings flit across his face. Shock, annoyance and something very like guilt.

'What are you talking about, Holly?' he growled. 'Where in the world did you get a ridiculous idea like that? I'm not going to marry Virginia.'

And yet there was some undertone in his voice, some note of reservation that made her feel she could not quite trust him.

'Aren't you?' she asked starkly.

'No, I'm not,' he said in a clipped tone that brooked no argument. 'Now, for heaven's sake, stop talking rubbish!'

But Holly wasn't going to let him get away that easily. Her anger surged up afresh.

'You needn't think you can just brush it aside like that as if it were some stupid suggestion at a meeting!' she cried. 'Damn it, Simon this is important. You cheated me and lied to me. You deceived me! All the time you were trying to chat me up, you were actually sleeping with Virginia!'

'I was what?' roared Simon. He turned and strode angrily across the room. 'Give me a break, Holly. I've never slept with Virginia in my life!'

'Don't lie to me!' cried Holly. 'Heaven knows, I practically caught you at it. I saw her coming out of your bed.'

'Out of my what?'

'Your bed,' insisted Holly. 'Well, your bedroom then. Your cabin on the paddlesteamer.'

'God almighty,' cried Simon. 'I don't believe this. Virginia came out of my cabin, so that proves I slept with her? Does it also prove I slept with you, my secretary and the woman who did the cleaning?'

Holly held on to her temper with difficulty.

'Don't play games with me, Simon, I know what I saw.'

'And what exactly did you see?' demanded Simon in a voice heavy with sarcasm.

Holly bit her lip and swallowed hard before she could reply.

'I saw Virginia coming out of your cabin at six o'clock on the last morning of the cruise.'

'Like hell you did,' exclaimed Simon. 'I never let anyone into my cabin at six o'clock in the morning. Well, not unless they're bringing me coffee or something.

That's my working time. Virginia couldn't possibly have been in...'

He stopped suddenly with an arrested expression on his face.

'What is it?' asked Holly.

He frowned and scratched his head.

'Now that you mention it,' he muttered, 'I think she did come into the cabin that morning. Only to ask me some damn fool question about the ratio of slaves to whites on the plantations in the eighteenth century. I told her to get the hell out and quit bugging me.'

Holly gave a bitter groan of laughter. It sounded so much like Simon she was almost convinced. And then she remembered how Virginia had looked.

'But she was wearing satin pyjamas,' she stammered. 'With the top button undone and her hair was all rumpled.'

'I don't care if she was wearing a penguin suit,' snapped Simon in exasperation. 'I didn't sleep with her, Holly. If she told you I did, she was just trying to make trouble between us.'

Holly paused in a torment of doubt. It was certainly true that Virginia disliked her and might be only too happy to cause problems for her. But what about the letter?

'But you asked her to marry you!' she insisted. 'She showed me the letter. It was there in black and white in your own handwriting.'

Simon looked suddenly shaken out of his composure. His black eyebrows drew together in a menacing scowl and he swore softly under his breath.

'That——!' he exclaimed. 'So she kept my letter, did she? I asked her to burn it.'

Holly felt suddenly as exhausted and wretched as if she had just run a marathon. She collapsed onto the couch with a choking sound deep in the back of her throat.

'Then it is true,' she said dully. 'You did write and ask her to marry you. You did say that you loved her.'

'No,' growled Simon swiftly. 'I never told her I loved her. Just the opposite. I told her I didn't.'

'I saw it there in black and white,' retorted Holly contemptuously.

'Well, I can't imagine how. Because when I wrote asking her to marry me, I distinctly said that I didn't love her, and I never would. In any case it's all over now.'

Holly stared at him, appalled.

'I don't understand,' she said. 'Why did you ask her to marry you, then, if you didn't love her?'

Simon gave a short laugh.

'Blame it on my upbringing!' he said. 'I didn't feel that love had any particular connection with marriage. Although to do him justice, my father tried to talk me out of that view.'

'Your father sounds like a fine man,' said Holly wryly. 'I'd really like to meet him some day.'

Simon looked at her with a strange expression.

'You already have,' he replied.

'What?'

She was startled, and her brain began to race. Then, like pieces clicking into place in a jigsaw puzzle, the answer suddenly became clear.

'You mean... Paul?'

Simon nodded.

'That's right. Although, as I told you before, he doesn't want it generally known. But I think he'd like you to be in on the secret.'

Holly sighed.

'I can't think why you say that!' she retorted bitterly. 'It makes it sound as though I have some special relationship with you. Some right to know your most private feelings and secrets. But I don't, do I, Simon? There's nothing in the least bit special between us.'

'Isn't there?' asked Simon, dropping on to the couch beside her. 'Then what am I doing here, Holly?'

'I don't know!' she cried angrily. 'I wish to heaven I did.'

Simon reached up and touched her cheek with a controlled urgency that made her heart skip a beat.

'Listen,' he said. 'You told me once that I was going too fast for you and I'm beginning to think you were right. Well, tell me this. Was the only reason you ran out on me because of Virginia's lies?'

'Yes,' admitted Holly.

'Then can't we start over again? Renew our friendship, get to know each other without any pressures?'

The silence lengthened agonisingly. Holly still had a lot of unanswered questions and she couldn't rid herself of the fear that Simon was merely playing with her. But as she looked at his narrowed blue eyes and brooding mouth, she knew with a surge of panic and exhilaration what her answer would be.

'Tell me, Mr Madigan,' she said formally, 'do you have any catering jobs coming up that I could do for you?'

His face lit up.

'Sure. I'm giving a special dinner for Paul in two weeks' time to celebrate a music award he's won. Maybe you'd like to handle that.'

A slow smile spread over Holly's face.

'Maybe I would.'

'There are two conditions, though.'

'Oh. What are they?' asked Holly.

'First, that you let me pay for the repairs to the restaurant.'

'I couldn't possibly——' began Holly, but the stern look on Simon's face quelled her. 'And second?'

'Second, that you help me paint this town red.'

* * *

The next two weeks were a bittersweet time for Holly. Although she was busy most evenings in the restaurant, they spent two unforgettable, toe tapping nights in Bourbon Street jazz clubs and they made the most of the daylight hours. Sailing on Lake Ponchartrain, sipping drinks in the revolving bar at the Top of the Mart restaurant thirty-three floors above the city, shopping in the Jax Brewery complex, riding around the town together in a horse-drawn surrey, soaking up all the colour and fun of *The Big Easy*. Holly could no longer deny even to herself that she was falling passionately in love with Simon and there were moments when she was convinced that he felt the same way about her. Moments when he looked at her with an expression that made her heart turn over. And yet he was maddeningly secretive and close-mouthed when it came to putting his feelings into words. Sometimes when he kissed her she felt the world spin away from her in an ecstatic blur of sensation. But although she was conscious of a mounting sexual tension between them, Simon kept his feelings on a tight leash. All the same, she could not doubt how much he wanted her. There were moments when she would glance up and find him gazing at her with a searing expression that made her shiver with unsatisfied yearnings. And there were moments when he seemed on the brink of saying something, something tremendously important but then he would turn the conversation into another channel with a joke or some casual, meaningless remark. Holly felt as if she were trapped on a pendulum, swinging between the extremes of rapturous bliss and a deep, corrosive anxiety. Did Simon really love her? Or was this just a slow, deliberate prelude to an elaborate seduction?

At least there were some compensations. Thanks to Simon's money and influence, the restaurant had now been totally repaired, so there was no longer the nagging worry of being closed down by the local government authority. A few days' rest had made Joel's back as good as new and he was now at the piano again each evening. And, best of all, Holly had had a letter from Heather in Hawaii, which was cautious and hesitant, yet obviously simmering with happiness. On the plane trip to Honolulu, Heather had been sitting next to a lawyer, who was thirty-six years old and widowed with two daughters a little older than Amber. He had been really kind and helpful to her and they had gone out to dinner several times in Honolulu. He wanted to keep dating her when they returned to New Orleans. What did Holly think about it? Holly gave an exultant whoop of delight and tossed the letter into the air. She thought it was wonderful!

Yet the one real worry which clouded this time for her was the continuing presence of Virginia in Simon's house. Holly had half hoped that he would ask her to leave, but he didn't seem to think of Virginia as anything other than a minor irritation, who would soon be gone anyway. In fact she was due to fly home the day after the dinner so that she could prepare her classes for the autumn term. Holly couldn't wait for the moment to come. Somehow she felt certain that everything would change between her and Simon once the dinner was over. And it did. But not quite in the way Holly had expected.

At Simon's insistence, she arrived early on the day of the dinner so that they could spend a couple of hours together looking over the house and the grounds. It was an amazingly beautiful place, with its fine antique furniture, landscaped gardens, views of the river and its rich sense of tradition. Simon showed her everything, from the carved eighteenth-century rice bed in the main bedroom to the small house or *garçonnière* in the grounds where he had lived while his mother was alive. They ate a lazy lunch of French bread, ham and salad together in a summerhouse under the shade of the big magnolia tree and later sat on a swing on the front porch, rocking dreamily back and forwards, with their shoulders touching. At last Holly announced reluctantly that it was time for her to go and start preparing the meal. Simon rose to his feet, rested his hands on her shoulders and looked down into her eyes.

'I shouldn't have let you talk me into this,' he said. 'I don't like the idea of you acting the servant to me. This is the last time you're ever to wait on me, you hear, Holly?'

Holly grinned and tickled his ribs playfully.

'What are you trying to do, put me out of business?' she complained.

But Simon didn't join in the joke. His eyes were narrowed and serious as he continued to look at her.

'Maybe I am,' he agreed.

It was seven-thirty when the guests began to arrive and Holly, taking a quick peek from the shelter of the dining-room, saw that they seemed to be exactly the same crowd who had been present on the first occasion. Virginia, Paul, the musicians from the river cruise, the two photographers and a lot of other people whom she still didn't know. But how different things were this time! Then, she had been nervous, apprehensive, half convinced that she hated Simon. This time she felt relaxed, confident, almost as much at ease as if she were in her own home and she knew with a sudden feeling of breathlessness that she loved Simon with her entire heart.

Before long she could hear the babble of voices and the clink of glasses from the living room, but she was too absorbed in her work to pay much attention. Her hands flew over her tasks, and soon the air was filled with the rich smell of seafood gumbo, beef filet marchand de vin and stuffed potatoes. The chocolate mousse for dessert was already in the fridge, so all she had to do now was make a green salad. At eight o'clock precisely, she made her way into the dining-room with the first trayful of food and set it on the serving table.

To her surprise and pleasure, Paul jumped up from his seat at once, came across to her, and kissed her warmly on both cheeks.

'Good to see you again, *chérie*,' he said. 'You come out and visit me again soon, eh?'

There was also a chorus of friendly greetings from the musicians and photographers who had been aboard the paddlesteamer and Simon smiled at her with an expression that made her flush and look away. In fact, the only thing that troubled her was the unmistakable hostility of Virginia who gave her a sharp, bitter look as Holly set down the bowl in front of her. The sense of antagonism that emanated from the other woman was so strong that it gave Holly a deep, ominous sense of misgiving. And yet what could Virginia do to hurt her after all? She would be on a plane back to upstate New York the following day and Holly and Simon would be left alone to shape their future. Virginia was powerless to hurt her.

Or so she thought. But she was wrong as she found out when Simon called her back into the dining-room at the end of the meal.

'Come and join us, Holly,' he invited, waving a bottle of Bollinger champagne. 'I've got an announcement to make and I want you to join in the celebration.'

With a puzzled smile, Holly accepted a glass of champagne and watched as Simon raised his own glass and looked around the assembled guests.

'First of all,' he said. 'I'd like you to drink a toast to Paul, whose album *Cajun Fiddler* has just topped the US charts for folk music recordings in the last month.'

They all raised their glasses and drank and Paul beamed at them.

'And secondly——' began Simon.

'Secondly,' cut in Virginia, rising to her feet and raising her glass, 'we want you all to drink a toast to Simon and me. We're making a formal announcement of our engagement and we'll be married next month.'

CHAPTER ELEVEN

FOR AN instant, Holly was too stunned to speak. A cold feeling of shock and disbelief clenched her insides and her feet seemed glued to the carpet so she couldn't move. Then suddenly speech and action came hurtling back to her. With a violent sweep of her arm, she flung her glass away from her so that it shattered loudly against the wall with a loud, detonating noise. Everyone gasped and Paul rose to his feet and came towards her, while Virginia simply stood and smirked triumphantly. But Holly had eyes for no one except Simon, who stood with a tight mouth and a face as expressionless as marble. A stab of pure torment went through her and she had to clench her hands at her sides to stop them from shaking.

'You bastard,' she breathed. 'You lying, deceitful——'

Her voice broke and she could not go on. With a sudden choking wail, she turned and fled from the room to the safety of the kitchen. Blinded by tears, she held on to the countertop for support and slumped forward, sobbing frantically, without a thought for who might hear her. Suddenly there was a faint rush of air, a firm footfall. Holly spun round, lashing out with her arms.

'Get away from me, Simon,' she cried. 'Don't touch me. Don't even come near me.'

But it wasn't Simon. It was Paul. His tanned face was creased into an expression of bewilderment and his brown eyes were full of pity. Ignoring her distraught weeping and her incoherent utterances, he took two steps closer and enfolded her in a gigantic bear hug.

'There, there, *chérie*,' he murmured, thumping her on the back and hugging her close. 'What's all this foolishness? It can't be true, what she says. You know it can't be true. Simon would never do such a thing to you.'

Holly raised a tear-blotched face to his and took a long, shuddering breath.

'Wouldn't he?' she demanded. 'Well, why didn't he explain, then? Why didn't he say something? Why did he just stand there and let her... let her...'

She broke into a fresh bout of wailing. Paul heaved a gusty sigh, shook his head and thumped her energetically on the back again.

'I don't know,' he admitted. 'But I'm sure as hell going in there to find out. Now you stay here and don't go away. There must be some reasonable explanation for all this.'

He patted her consolingly on the cheek, gave her one final hug and strode purposefully out of the room with a scowl on his face that reminded her of Simon.

Left alone, Holly experienced a strange sense of anticlimax and gazed about her helplessly, feeling disoriented. What was she to do? She couldn't stand here all evening crying her heart out. And yet the moment she thought of Simon and Virginia a fresh bout of weeping threatened to overtake her. Ruthlessly, she turned on the cold tap, cupped her hands and splashed the pure water all over her face. It made her shudder, but it did her good. Tearing off a length of kitchen towel, she dried her eyes, dabbed at the wet skin and blew her nose. Then she washed her hands and for lack of anything better to do, mechanically began to tidy up the kitchen. The habits of a lifetime were strong. The world might have come to an end this evening, but she still couldn't go home and leave a pot encrusted with shrimp gumbo completely unwashed.

A strange sense of unreality came over her as she moved about the kitchen doing the soothing, familiar tasks. Scraping plates, rinsing and stacking, loading the dishwasher, putting pots to soak in the huge sink, and all the while she felt as if she had pressed the pause button on her thoughts, making them hang suspended so that she did not have to watch them unroll in their full horror. Dimly she became aware of a distant uproar going on in the living-room. Raised voices, slammed doors, the sound of argument. Then there were hurrying footsteps on the stairs. More footsteps, coming down. The noise of car engines starting up. Perhaps ten minutes passed. Or maybe it was ten years. And then he was there. Simon, standing in the kitchen doorway, his hands on his hips, blue eyes narrowed and piercing, his mouth twisted in a wry smile. She backed against the counter, but there was no escape. He strode across the room, seized her by the shoulders and gazed hungrily down at her.

'I guess this isn't the best time in the world to tell you I love you and want to marry you,' he said with a question in his voice.

Holly closed her eyes and gave a half hysterical gasp of laughter.

'When you've just became engaged to another woman?' she sneered. 'You're damn right it isn't!'

Jerking out of his hold, she tried to flee across to the other side of the kitchen, but he grabbed her arm and spun her round to face him.

'Look at me,' he commanded. 'It's not true. Virginia made up that ridiculous announcement. She only said it to try and drive you away.'

'What?' Holly screwed up her face in bewilderment. 'I don't understand.'

Simon sighed heavily.

'Then I guess it's time I told you the whole, rotten story.'

'Don't tell me anything,' cried Holly. 'We're finished! Don't you understand? Finished.'

'No! Don't say that.'

With a determined movement, Holly walked across the room, tore off her apron and grabbed her handbag.

'You're wasting your time, Simon. I'm not going to listen to any more of your smooth-talking lies. You've got guests to attend to and I'm getting a taxi home.'

'My guests have all gone.'

'What about dear Virginia?'

Holly had meant it to sound jeering, but instead it came out in a pathetic wobble. Angrily she clamped her lips together to stop them from quivering.

'She's gone too. I couldn't let her stay on any longer after the trouble she caused. Paul's driven her to a hotel for the night. She'll fly back to New York State tomorrow morning and I hope to God that's the last time I ever see her.'

His voice was raw, angry, the words coming out like a hail of bullets. For a moment Holly was almost convinced then she bit hard on her lip and shook her head in anguish.

'I don't believe you,' she said bitterly.

'You must believe me,' insisted Simon pursuing her across the room and seizing her arms. 'Holly, you can't leave. That's exactly what Virginia wanted, to drive you away. She's been trying everything in the book, even threatening to sue me for breach of promise if I don't marry her. Well, let her try. I don't care. The only thing I care about is if I lose you.'

'But Simon, why should she try so hard?' demanded Holly. 'I don't understand. You told me it was all over between you.'

Simon winced.

'I thought it was,' he agreed. 'It certainly was for me. And I've never had any reason to think she cared a damn about me, in fact I'm still sure she doesn't. It's just that she's the kind of woman who likes to call the shots. She wanted to be in control, to be the one who dumped me, not the other way round. I should never have got involved with her in the first place.'

'Then why did you?' challenged Holly.

'I never intended to,' he retorted. 'At first I only spent time with her to be polite. My mother kept throwing us together because she hoped we'd eventually marry each other.'

'But why?' asked Holly. 'Why did she want you to marry?'

'Oh, it's impossible to explain! My mother had a lot of good qualities but I have to admit that deep down she was an incredible snob. When Virginia wrote last summer and asked if she could research a book about plantation owners that centred on our property, she was thrilled. And once she found out that Virginia's family came over to the States on the Mayflower and had old money and good family connections, nothing would do for her but she must throw us together and try to get us to marry. I thought it was a bit of a joke really, but I was happy enough to show up and eat dinner with Virginia if that was what my mother wanted. Then one night my mother went to bed early, deliberately leaving Virginia and me alone in the dining-room. With all the right trappings. Candlelight, a Mozart sonata playing on the stereo in the background, moonlight over the water. You can imagine. But I can't believe that dear Mama had any real idea of the kind of proposal Virginia was going to put to me.'

'Proposal?' echoed Holly. 'Did she ask you to marry her?'

'No,' growled Simon, and his face was suddenly hard and dangerous and unforgiving. 'Something entirely different was on her mind. She told me quite frankly that she wanted a child. She was thirty-five years old, time was running out and she needed someone to father it. So she had picked on me as a likely candidate. After all, as she told me, I was moderately intelligent, I came from a good family and I had money and a nice, straight nose. Put bluntly, Virginia wanted me to act as a stud for her.'

Holly recoiled in dismay.

'That's horrible,' she exclaimed.

Simon nodded bitterly.

'Yes, it was horrible,' he agreed. 'I thought I was pretty hard-boiled, but it was too much even for me to stomach. My first response was that she didn't mean it, it was all a joke. I burst out laughing. And then I realised she was serious. I can't remember exactly how I felt then, but certainly humiliated, used, angry. Of course I said no. But afterwards, after she'd gone back to New York State, I began to think.'

Holly stared at him in dismay.

'Surely you didn't agree to it?' she demanded.

'Not exactly,' he said in a surly voice. 'After all, I knew first-hand about the pain of a child growing up without its real father. But on the other hand, when I really thought about it, I realised I wanted kids too. And a home. Besides, my mother was right in a way. Virginia and I did have some things in common, even if it was only money, property and a certain type of background. I started to think it might work, even though I didn't love her, so I wrote and asked her to marry me.'

'And that was the letter I read?' prompted Holly.

Simon sighed.

'I guess so.'

Holly was silent for a moment, digesting these new revelations. The whole arrangement repelled her, it was so calculating, so lacking in feeling. And yet at the same time she couldn't help feeling a certain sympathy with Simon. At least he had tried to do the honourable thing, by asking Virginia to marry him. Holly almost felt an unwilling admiration for him and then she remembered the contents of that hurtful letter.

'But you said you loved her!' she cried accusingly.

'No, I didn't,' he protested. 'I said exactly the opposite. I told her I didn't.'

Holly gave a gasp of impatience.

'I've read the letter, Simon,' she insisted.

Simon swore under his breath.

'Look, I'll prove it to you,' he announced. 'I know I kept a copy of that letter somewhere; heaven knows I must have done a dozen drafts of it before I finally sent it off. I'll find the whole thing and show it to you in black and white.'

Grabbing Holly's hand, he dragged her ruthlessly out of the kitchen across the hall and into his study. Unlocking an antique walnut escritoire, he began rummaging inside, and at last pulled out a folder full of papers. Half a dozen letters fell on to the desk, most of them full of scratchings out. Then he picked up one clean copy and thrust it at Holly.

'There! That's it!' he said. 'Read it for yourself.'

Casting him a suspicious look, Holly accepted the two sheets of paper and scanned them swiftly. It was immediately obvious that the second page was an exact copy of the document Virginia had shown her. But the first page was completely new to her and as she read swiftly through it, she saw that it changed the meaning of the entire letter. Clearing her throat, she began to read aloud.

Dear Virginia,

I have thought further about your extraordinary proposal and, to be honest, I still find it as repellent as ever. No child should be the product of such cold-hearted, calculating conception nor grow up without knowing its true father.

But, as you said we're both mature adults and know what we're getting into, so I have a different proposal to make to you. Why don't we get married, have a child and try to make a genuine success of it? Of course it won't be easy. It isn't as if...

At this point, the writing went on to the next page and began again with the words Holly had read before.

'I'm in love with you, Virginia, and I don't believe my feelings will ever change.

'Now do you believe me?' challenged Simon.

Holly nodded slowly.

'It changes everything,' she admitted. 'So you really did tell her that you didn't love her?'

'That's right,' agreed Simon.

'But how could you bear to propose to her, then?' burst out Holly. 'That's horrible, it's so cold, so calculating, so unfeeling!'

Simon winced. 'I know,' he admitted. 'I'm not proud of myself. But you must remember my upbringing, Holly. I had an awful lot of anger and pain and fear of commitment churning around inside me. I guess that's what made me so cynical.'

'But if she wanted a child and you offered to marry her, why didn't it happen then?'

Simon gave an impatient sigh and ran his fingers through his dark hair.

'After Virginia received my letter, she phoned me back with a counter-offer. Yes, I know, I know! Don't pull faces like that, Holly. It does sound like one of my business deals, doesn't it? But that's the whole point. That's what I wanted or thought I wanted—a cool, sensible, safe arrangement. Until I met you.'

Holly stiffened warily. Simon wasn't going to get away with it that easily!

'What was her... counter-offer?' she challenged.

'Well, she said she wasn't at all sure that marriage was what she wanted, but she was prepared to think about it. She suggested that she should come down here to stay again this summer while we both figured out what we wanted. And, until we did, neither of us should consider ourselves bound in any way. That sounded fair enough to me, so I agreed. But the whole thing was a farce from start to finish.'

'What do you mean?' asked Holly uncertainly.

'It's obvious, isn't it? I thought I was hard-boiled enough to marry a woman I didn't love, but only because I hadn't yet met the one I did. And when I did meet you, Holly, you knocked my plans all out of kilter!

After I kissed you that first evening here, I was so wound up I knew it would be crazy to marry Virginia. I didn't know how the hell I was going to handle you, but I was sure of one thing. I couldn't marry her.'

'So what did you do?' prompted Holly. 'Did you tell her?'

Simon gritted his teeth.

'Yes. No. I told her some of it. Not how I felt about you, because I didn't understand it myself, and anyway it was too intense, too private. But I told her that I didn't think we should get married after all. That it wouldn't work for either of us.'

'And w-what did she say?' faltered Holly.

'She was very calm about it. You know that cool, rather superior smile that she has? Well, she smiled like that and said I was probably right.'

'That's all?'

'Yes. I was rather taken aback by it, but I was also relieved. Obviously she wasn't suffering from a broken heart or anything.'

'But, Simon, why did she stay here once you'd told her the marriage was off? Why didn't she just go back home?'

Simon's face wore a hunted look.

'I wish she had now!' he said grimly. 'But at the time it didn't seem to matter. She was so calm, so amused, almost indifferent about it. And she wanted to stay and finish the research for her book. She was also doing some statistical analysis for me on a contract basis. Of course I had no idea that she was going to spring that announcement on us tonight!'

'But why did she?' persisted Holly. 'If she doesn't really love you herself?'

'Mainly out of spite,' said Simon, 'judging by what she has just told me. Her pride is hurt. She feels offended that I could prefer "a penniless kitchenmaid", as she puts it, to her, and she's outraged that I've fallen in love with you, whereas I never fell in love her. And in some crazy way I think she felt my offer remained open until she chose to refuse it, no matter what I had said to her. Apart from that, I guess she may have found it hard to find another moderately intelligent man, with money and a nice straight nose, who wanted to sire her child.'

Holly shuddered at the hard edge of sarcasm in his voice.

'Can she really sue you?' she asked.

'I doubt if she'll bother,' he replied. 'If she does, I've enough lawyers and money to deal with it. But damn Virginia, I don't care if she sues me, I don't care what she does. All I care about is you.'

The cold, bitter mask of his face suddenly softened. His blue eyes kindled and he reached out one lean, brown finger and touched her cheek.

'Truly?' asked Holly unsteadily.

'Truly,' insisted Simon.

Threading his fingers through her hair, he drew her against him.

'I wanted you from the first moment I saw you. But I didn't realise how much you'd got under my skin until I walked into the saloon on the paddlesteamer and saw you kissing John. Holly, what did happen between you and John?'

With dancing eyes and a delicious sense of apprehension, Holly told him. Simon swore softly and shook his head.

'I should have known,' he sighed. 'From the first time I set eyes on you, I had a terrible suspicion you spelled trouble. I thought you were sassy, opinionated and crazy enough to drive a man wild.'

'So when did you decide that you loved me?' she asked with a catch in her voice.

He frowned and memories seemed to flash before his eyes.

'Probably that night in Paul's cabin,' he said, 'although I didn't want to admit it to myself at first. It scared the hell out of me to find that I could actually need somebody so much. And I still wasn't sure that what I actually craved was marriage until——'

'Until?'

'That day I saw you in the market with Amber and I thought she was yours. It jolted the hell out of me. I'd never imagined that I could feel such an outpouring of rage, jealousy, compassion, desire as I felt towards you. Then I suddenly realised it didn't matter to me whose kid Amber was. If she was yours, I'd learn to love her, just the way I loved you. And marriage seemed the only institution grand enough, safe enough, permanent enough for what I wanted to offer you.'

'Oh, Simon,' breathed Holly, blinking back tears.

'How about you?' he asked. 'What did you feel towards me?'

She bit her lip and smiled mistily.

'When I first met you I thought you were cold, ruthless, arrogant and mean,' she replied.

'Thanks,' said Simon drily.

Holly burrowed her head into his chest and rubbed her cheek against his shirt. Then she looked up at him, halfway between tears and laughter.

'Until I discovered that you're also kind to kids, passionate, generous, reliable in a crisis, one hell of a pianist and the best kisser in the whole world,' she added.

Simon's face lit up.

'Is that so?' he demanded hoarsely.

Dragging her even harder against him, he kissed her with a passion that left her breathless. At last, tilting back her head so she could look at him, she posed the question that had suddenly begun to trouble her.

'Simon, what did you say when you first came into the kitchen?'

For a moment he looked blank and then an understanding gleam came into his eyes. Obediently, he repeated his earlier words.

'I said, I guess this isn't the best time to tell you I'm in love with you and want to marry you.'

'Try it,' challenged Holly.

'Holly,' he demanded in a tone that was far closer to an order rather than a request. 'Are you going to marry me?'

She leaned forward and flung her arms around his neck.

'Of course I am, Simon,' she cried gladly.

'Right,' growled Simon. 'Then there's only one thing to be done.'

With a ruthless lunge, he caught her in his arms and swept her into the air as effortlessly as if she were a doll. Then he went racing out into the hallway and bounded up the stairs until he reached the main bedroom. Kicking open the door, he strode across the room and dropped her right in the middle of the huge, carved bed. His breath was coming in a fast, uneven rhythm and his eyes glittered strangely as he looked down at her. Crouching above her, he smoothed back her tumbled hair from her face and let his warm, strong hand trail down the column of her throat and over the swelling mound of her breast. Holly felt her whole body throb into violent, pulsating life and she turned her head and deposited a small, quivering kiss on the inside of his arm.

He looked at her with a question blazing in his eyes and with barely a pause she nodded.

'I told you once I'd wait until you were ready,' he muttered hoarsely. 'Do you think——?'

'Yes,' she whispered.

Wordlessly he gazed down at her with an intensity that made her pulses throb tumultuously. Then with a swift, tense motion he rose to his feet and began tearing off his clothes in blind abandonment. She gave a soft groan low in the throat at the sight of his naked body in the dim glow of the hall light. He was quite simply magnificent. Broad, square shoulders and a massive chest tapered to a narrow waist, athletic hips and long, powerful legs. As he moved towards her, she saw his muscles bunch and ripple under the satiny gleam of his tanned skin. But it was not just the strength and sheer animal magnetism of his body that aroused her. It was the look on his face. A deep, compelling hunger was mingled with a tenderness so urgent that she gave a tremulous sigh of satisfaction as he sat down on the bed beside her.

'Do you really love me, Simon?' she breathed.

'More than I can tell you,' he assured her earnestly. 'I wanted you from the first moment I saw you, Holly. And the more I got to know you, the more I realised that it wasn't just desire. I want everything from you, Holly. Love. Sex. Passion. Marriage. Children. A whole lifetime of commitment. Will you give me all that?'

His face contorted and a spasm of muscular tension clenched his hands on the bedspread. As he gazed down at her, the thought flitted through her mind that a man going crazy with thirst in a desert would look like that when he found water. Incredulous. Joyful. Desperate for reassurance that what he saw was real. Holly swallowed hard and reached up to touch his face.

'Yes,' she said huskily.

'Then, for the love of providence, let me get that damned dress off you before I go crazy.'

She giggled weakly as his merciless fingers tore open the buttons and he hauled her into a sitting position. The dress was dragged violently over her head and flung into a far corner of the room with riotous abandon. A moment later her underwear followed suit. But when she was quite naked, she no longer felt like laughing. For Simon lay beside her and hauled her against him, threading his hands through her hair and burying his face in her neck. He took a long, deep breath, as if inhaling her very essence.

'I love you, Holly,' he growled. 'More than you'll ever imagine. And I'm going to make you mine. All mine.'

Seizing her by the chin, he turned her face up to his and kissed her so fiercely that she whimpered. And yet the warm, urgent thrust of his tongue, the hard, insistent pressure of his body on hers woke an aching need deep inside her. Arching her back, she lifted her lips invitingly to his and snuggled closer into his hold. Her breasts brushed against the powerful bulge of his chest muscles and he gave a groan low in his throat.

'You little witch. Come here.'

Tumbling her into the centre of the bed, he set his lips to the place where a pulse throbbed tumultuously in her neck. Then with a thoroughness that left her gasping he began to kiss his way down the entire length of her body. The sensations that thrilled through her at his touch were almost too explosive to endure. The moist, teasing caress of his lips and tongue sent ripples of fire into every crevice and nerve-ending. And when he reached the secret, innermost part of her, she felt a dark, mysterious heat surge through her. A low cry broke from her lips and she tried to struggle up, to take some part in this extraordinary ecstasy that was beginning to blaze between them. She had never dreamt such sensations were possible, would have died if Dennis had done such a thing to her. But Dennis had only ever cared about his own pleasure, while Simon was wholly absorbed in hers.

'Lie still, honey,' he murmured hoarsely. 'And let it happen.'

With a faint whimper, she let him push her back against the pillows. But now even the crisp touch of cotton against her skin seemed to be too much to endure as the relentless, tormenting caresses continued. A throbbing ache began to pulse in her loins and fever blazed through her veins. Her eyelids drooped, her breathing grew fast and shallow and her head began to thresh violently from side to side. Wanton images flashed like lightning in her mind, but nothing could be so wanton as the reality of what was happening to her. Simon. Simon. The man whom she loved with her whole heart and being who was really here in the bed with her. She could smell the sharp, primitive tang of aroused male, hear the harsh, irregular rhythm of his breathing, feel the exquisite, unendurable touch of his lips... Suddenly the sensations building inside her mounted to an abrupt, driving climax and she felt her whole body clench as if she could grip this moment and hold it safe forever.

'Simon. Oh. Simon.'

Her cry was little more than a moan, so distorted it was barely audible. But he heard it and knew what it signified. Flattening himself into a low crouch, he moved forward until his body covered hers. Then he lowered himself on to her so that she was crushed beneath the full, satisfying warmth of his muscular frame. Her eyes fluttered open, shooting little darts of light like reflections from a turbulent pool.

'I love you, Simon,' she whispered.

'I love you too, Holly.'

Just to hear him say it was almost enough to bring tears to her eyes. But to hear him say it with that smouldering urgency in his voice made her spirits soar. Reaching up, she caressed his temples and heard him give a faint groan at her touch. Suddenly he seized her fingers, planted a burning kiss on them and gazed down at her with a fierce question in his eyes.

'Holly,' he rasped. 'I can't wait another moment. Do you think——'

'Yes, my darling. Yes, oh yes.'

Her body shifted under his and she moved to welcome him, glorying in the sudden, hard, uncompromising thrust of his masculinity. He was so powerful, so warm, so full of passion and vigour. With a soft sigh of fulfilment, she closed her eyes and nuzzled her face into his shoulder. And as their rhythm became faster, stronger, more urgent, the boundaries between them seemed to burst and a sense of total union engulfed her. Stars exploded behind her eyes and she soared into a mystic region where she and Simon were one.

It was a long time before she came back to earth. Simon was still lying on top of her, spent and shuddering, his breathing coming slowly and his lips resting dreamily against her cheek. But when her eyelids fluttered open, he raised his head and looked down at her out of narrowed blue eyes. Outside the moon had risen and its milky radiance reflected off the silver curves of the Mississippi River and glanced in through the uncurtained window. In its shimmering glow, Simon's face looked haunted and strange with an indefinable hint of regret around the mouth.

'What are you thinking?' asked Holly sharply, gripped by a sudden dread.

'That I wish I hadn't wasted so many years of my life before I found you. And that now I've got you, I want to make the most of it. How soon can we be married, Holly?'

Holly laughed out loud with relief.

'The sooner, the better,' she replied, lifting her lips to his.

Full of Eastern Passion...

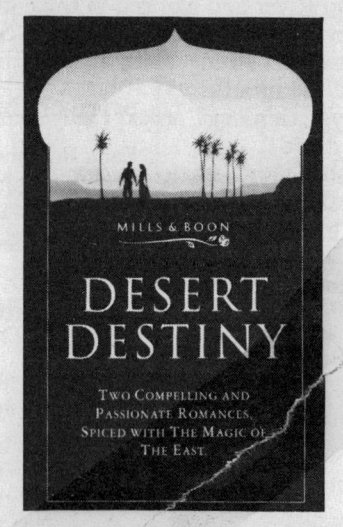

MILLS & BOON

DESERT DESTINY

TWO COMPELLING AND PASSIONATE ROMANCES, SPICED WITH THE MAGIC OF THE EAST.

Savour the romance of the East this summer with our two full-length compelling Romances, wrapped together in one exciting volume.

AVAILABLE FROM 29 JULY 1994   PRICED £3.99

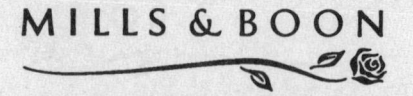

MILLS & BOON

Available from WH Smith, John Menzies, Volume One, Forbuoys, Martins, Woolworths, Tesco, Asda, Safeway and other paperback stockists. Also available from Mills & Boon Reader Service, FREEPOST, PO Box 236, Croydon, Surrey CR9 9EL. (UK Postage & Packing free)